NUCLEAR ATTACK

a novel by

Richard G. Edwards

Cover Photo
The photograph on the cover is the 1954 Castle Romeo nuclear test firing on Bikini Atoll in the Central Pacific's Marshall Islands. It is from the National Nuclear Security Administration/Nevada Field Office. The iconic mushroom cloud was created from a huge 4 megaton yield. The image has come to epitomize nuclear explosions.

Acknowledgements

I am sincerely indebted to several people who took the time and made the effort to review the manuscript for this novel. Dr. Bill Green, Mr. Jack Sterling, Dr. Gus Peters, and my wife Carolyn provided many excellent suggestions, comments, and corrections. The expert layout of the book was provided by Mrs. Kelly Elliott. Thanks so much to each of you. Pax Tecum!

Dedication

I have been abundantly blessed with many, many dear friends. I truly cherish each and every one. I can't start naming them for fear of leaving someone out! I have many friends in Harlan, Kentucky and fellow graduates from Harlan High School, class of 1958. A more recent group of friends meets here in Lexington every Friday for lunch. We started doing this over 25 years ago and are still at it. We now call ourselves the ROMEOs, **R**etired **O**ld **M**en **E**ating **O**ut! From my working years I have many friends from the University of Kentucky College of Engineering, and a group of retirees from there meets monthly for lunch. And I have many, many friends at my current church, Anchor Baptist here in Lexington, and from previous churches through the years. I dedicate this book to all my friends.....what would life be without them? Pax Tecum!

Preface

I recently finished the fifth and what I thought would be my final book. The five novels constitute **The Anchor Cross Series**. My good friend, fellow author, and fellow Harlan High School graduate, Mr. Bill J. Looney, finally convinced me a few years back to try my hand at writing novels. I remember Bill telling me, "You won't make any money at it, but it sure is a lot of fun." He was right on both counts!! So after finishing **The Anchor Cross Series**, I had the idea for **Nuclear Attack** rolling around in my head and decided to lose some more money and have some more fun by writing it. I hope you enjoy the read, and I'd certainly like to hear from you. Send any comments to

RICHARDGLENNEDWARDS@GMAIL.COM

Should you be interested in my Anchor Cross Series novels they are available at Amazon.com and at BarnesandNoble.com or by contacting me at my email address listed above. The titles of the novels are as follows:

#1 ***The Anchor Cross Second Edition***
#2 ***The Pelle Anchor Cross***
#3 ***The Helena Anchor Cross***
#4 ***The Anchor Cross Twins***
#5 ***The Constantine Anchor Cross***

Chapter 1

Washington, D.C.
The White House
December 1

Dickson Cannon, President of the United States, stared intently at the two other people sitting at the conference table. To his left sat Jon Kennan, Director of the Central Intelligence Agency, and to his right Susan Bean, Director of National Intelligence. President Cannon did not look happy.

"Kim's nothing but an ass," President Cannon said in reference to North Korea's Supreme Leader, Kim Jong-un. "The little fat-ass dictator does nothing but stir up trouble. He spends all his country's money on himself and his rag-tag army, leaving his people to starve to death. We should have taken him out years ago. His grandfather and father were almost as bad. We knew they had nuclear weapons, and we knew Kim was stupid enough to use them. So tell me why we now have this situation?"

Susan Bean looked toward Jon Kennan to respond. Keenan reported to Bean.

"Mr. President," replied Director Keenan, "it's just one of those situations where a mistake was made at the very beginning. There should never have been a North and South Korea. We had the chance after the Korean war to prevent the formation of the two nations, but we blew it. It's been downhill with North Korea ever since. I think the time has come for us to take the steps to eliminate him."

"Easier said than done, Mr. Director," President Cannon replied, "at least without starting World War III. I do agree we need to develop a plan to accomplish his demise, but before we can get to that we have to deal with this immediate problem."

Susan Bean reflected on what had brought about the present meeting. Reliable intelligence sources had reported to Jon Keenan that North Korea was actively engaged in plans for a nuclear attack on the United States on January 8th, Kim Jong-un's birthday. According to the sources, Kim had ordered the strike as a birthday present to himself.

Susan Bean said, "The good thing is we know about it. And if we know about it, we can prevent it."

The President responded, "We only know some things. Today is December 1, so we know we have about 38 days to stop him. We know he plans to bomb Los Angeles via a ship launch outside our territorial limits in the Pacific. We know he has nuclear warheads and we know that he has the missiles to deliver them from that short range. That we do know. And we don't apparently know a hell of a lot more than that. So, Directors, pray tell how we stop this maniac from killing millions of Americans and starting World War III?"

"Thank goodness we do have what we believe to be solid intelligence on how he plans to deliver the strike," replied Director Bean. "We know North Korea has chartered a commercial ship from a private Japanese company and will use it to carry the weapon system. They have told the Japanese they have a cargo shipment of goods to go to Venezuela. I feel sure they've worked something with the crooked Venezuela officials to vouch for them.   The North Koreans have also said that 12 of their people will be going with the shipment, saying they are needed to assemble the shipped goods upon arrival in Venezuela. All this info we learned from sources in the Japanese government, since the ship's trip had to be logged in advance. The ship will leave from a North Korean port on their east side and proceed east in the Sea of Japan and then across the Pacific. At some point in the trip the 12 North Koreans will commandeer the ship and force the Japanese crew to head toward Los Angeles rather than toward the Panama Canal. And then when they get suitably close they will weigh anchor and ready their missile system to fire the weapon. We think they have perfected a low altitude, surface skimming missile that can fly about 400 feet above the water or ground below it.....certainly low enough to avoid radar detection. We're not sure the speed of the missile, but it will not take long to reach its target."

"Why don't we just blow the hell out of the ship?" President Cannon asked.

"Couple of reasons," Susan Bean replied. "Number one, that would kill quite a number of innocent Japanese crew members. Number two, it could prompt retaliations that could set off World War III. And since the weapon system and the rest of the ship would be destroyed, we would have no proof of their intentions."

"Can't we just intercept the incoming missile?" the President asked.

Jon Keenan answered, "No, not if it flies below the radar. Can't find it."

"What about just having one or more of our fast attack ships there to board their boat when it gets ready to launch?" President Cannon asked.

"Likely couldn't do it fast enough, and they'd see us coming. We also thought about helicopters, but they too would be picked up on radar and would be heard. The North Koreans would also likely have some high caliber guns to defend themselves," said Director Bean. "And we also thought about ways to try and use our subs. But nothing seems workable."

"Okay. So what do we do?" said President Cannon.

Director Kennan replied, "As soon as we learned of Kim's plan we started scanning our data bases to see if we could locate one or more persons that we might be able to place on the Japanese vessel as crew that could abort the mission at the appropriate time. We wanted these people to be either Japanese or Korean and to have all the other training prerequisites necessary to accomplish such a mission. We found the best candidates to be among six North Korean soldiers recently granted political asylum and now living in Harlan County, Kentucky."

———————

In 325 AD Constantine the Great was emperor of Rome. He had converted to Christianity after being influenced greatly by his mother, Helena. Constantine had a dream, and in this dream he had a vision of a beautiful golden anchor cross that would symbolize the Christian religion. Prior to this time, and going back many centuries before Christ, the anchor was frequently used as a religious symbol. Hebrews 6:19 says, "We have this hope (meaning salvation through Christ) as an anchor of the soul, sure and steadfast." Until the time of Constantine the cross on which Christ was crucified was thought of in very negative terms because upon it only the worst criminals were placed. Perhaps in his vision Constantine was reminded of First Corinthians 1:18 that says, "For the message of the cross is foolishness to those who are perishing, but to us who are being saved it is the power of God." Constantine decided to share his vision with Pope Sylvester I who then told the emperor that he would give him a bar of very special gold from which he could mold his envisioned anchor cross. The bar of gold was one of many that had been blessed by the Lord and then given to Saint Peter to be used in establishing the church. It was called Saint Peter's gold. Constantine then gathered his most skilled craftsmen, described to them his anchor cross vision, and directed them to produce a mold which could be used to cast the golden anchor cross. This was done, and the result was a beautiful anchor cross about six inches high, four inches wide, and about one-half inch thick. The one bar of Saint Peter's gold was enough to produce six of the anchor crosses. Each had a hole in the top of the vertical arm of the cross that enabled a necklace to be threaded through so it could be worn about the neck. Also, on the horizontal arm was formed the words ***Pax Tecum***, Latin meaning "Peace be with you", a message from the one whom had blessed the gold, the Prince of Peace. The six anchor crosses were beautiful beyond belief. Constantine was delighted, and decided to keep one of them for himself and give the other five to Pope Sylvester I for the church to use as it decided appropriate.

Almost 16 years ago one of these anchor crosses was discovered in a remote location in the mountains of Eastern Kentucky by a child exploring in the woods. The boy, whose name was Kyle Potter, happened upon the ruins of a horse drawn wagon that had belonged to an early Harlan County, Kentucky pioneer named Reverend Karl Seibert, who, along with his wife Mary, were on their way in 1798 to the settlement called Mount Pleasant (later named Harlan) to start a church. The Seiberts had been attacked and killed by indians. Among the remains Kyle Potter recovered one of the golden anchor crosses. After showing the artifact to his mother she contacted their pastor, Raymond Bell, and he in turn contacted his friend in Lexington, Kentucky, Dr. Randy

Peters, the Director of the University of Kentucky's Center for Appalachian Research. Dr. Peters uncovered the history of the artifact, now being called the Seibert anchor cross, and discovered that there were five more that Constantine had produced. Then, after another 12 years, the second anchor cross was discovered in Prato, Italy where it had been placed in a church by its wealthy owner, Mr. Domenico Pelle. The remaining anchor crosses then began being discovered around the world. The third, the Helena anchor cross, was found in the Seychelles, the fourth and fifth were located in Madrid, Spain and were owned by twin sisters Elisabeth and Henriette Carmen, descendents in the lineage of French King Louis XV. The sixth and final anchor cross, the one that Constantine kept for himself, was found about 18 months ago by treasurer hunters diving off the Italian coast close to the island of Ponza. Having established himself as the world's leading authority on the anchor crosses, also called the Savior's crosses, Dr. Randy Peters had temporary possession of all six of the artifacts at his Lexington, Kentucky Center for Appalachian Research (CAR). The owners of the artifacts had all agreed to allow Dr. Peters to study them in an attempt to better understand their amazing history and characteristics. Each of the six anchor crosses had demonstrated numerous times amazing, unexplained power to protect from harm those possessing them. The media had reported world-wide the stories of each of these Savior's crosses, and their fame had even resulted in an annual October festival held in Harlan, Kentucky in their honor. The festival was called ACFes. Thousands flooded the streets of Harlan each year to view and celebrate the beautiful golden artifacts.

It was their world-wide media coverage that came to the attention of North Korea Supreme Leader Kim Jong-un. Kim was not impressed by their history, beauty, or their value. He was intrigued by the mysterious power they seemed to possess. He had a team of researchers study what was known about the artifacts, and after hearing that each anchor cross had indeed exhibited unexplained power to protect the wearer he commissioned a team of six of his best military people to travel to the United States with the mission to steal all six anchor crosses during their exhibition at the annual ACFes in Harlan, Kentucky. Kim was then prepared to send the team of six to Washington, D.C. to capture the White House and thus give him power over the U.S. Each man would be wearing one of the anchor crosses for protection, and therefore should be unstoppable to accomplish the mission. But when the soldiers attempted the theft, an unexpected event occurred that aborted their mission. Kim was furious, and executed many in his government that he held responsible for the failed attempt. The six North Koreans involved in the plot were taken under the wing of Harlan County Sheriff J. Bert Sterling. The sheriff recognized that the six were merely serving their despicable dictator, and that they would be executed if returned to North Korea. Also, Sheriff Sterling sensed that the six were basically very good people, just misdirected. So he managed to place them with two brothers, the Slusher Brothers, who agreed to allow them to work on their large Harlan County farm while their applications for political asylum were being processed.

The President looked solemnly at his two directors and said, "Do you two feel comfortable with that plan? Do you really think we can get one or more of those six North Korean soldiers to cooperate with us to disable the missile? Might they not still have allegiance to Kim and their native country?"

Susan Bean replied, "Mr. President, we've carefully considered all our options. We definitely think they will fully cooperate. Our people have had detailed discussions with Harlan County Sheriff Sterling. Of course we didn't tell him what Kim was up to, but we did make sure he knew the seriousness of the situation and that we had to be absolutely confident that the North Koreans could be trusted. He said that in both his professional and personal opinions he thought they would keep their allegiance to us. He said they all had really grown to love living in Harlan County and had been extremely good citizens. Also, after the six had applied for political asylum our agents visited with them to learn everything we could about their knowledge of the North Korean military and about Kim Jong-un. They were all extremely cooperative. Once their political asylum was granted they were really free to leave the Slusher brothers, but all unanimously wanted to stay. They said they were treated better than at any other time in their lives and felt it an honor to work for the brothers." Director Bean then looked at Director Kennan and said, "Jon and I highly recommend this course of action." Jon Kennan nodded affirmatively.

"Okay. You know the lives of millions of Americans and very likely the start of World War III will be riding on them," President Cannon said while still staring at the two. "So let's bring in the rest of the team and you two can present the situation and the proposed plan to them. We'll see if we can get agreement."

Jon Kennan stood and walked to the conference room door and opened it. Waiting outside were the secretaries of State, Defense, Energy, and Homeland Security along with the Chairman of the Joint Chiefs of Staff, the White House Chief of Staff, the Deputy National Security Advisor, Attorney General, Ambassador to the United Nations, and Homeland Security Advisor. The ten additional members of the United States National Security Council then joined the other three and they all took a seat.

President Cannon addressed the group, "Ladies and Gentlemen, I want to thank each of you for your cooperation to make this meeting on such short notice. We were really lucky that you were available. I realize that most of you likely had to cancel important meetings or events, but when you hear the seriousness of the subject at hand I know you'll understand my insistence for your attendance. I'll ask Director Jon Kennan to brief you on our situation. Jon."

Jon Kennan stood and walked to the front of the room where everyone could better see and hear him. He gave essentially the same briefing that he and Susan Bean had just given to the President. There were audible gasps heard from several when he explained Kim Jong-un's plan. All listened intently to his briefing. He then explained the proposed plan to defuse the intended strike. Several of the same questions raised by the President were asked, but in the end all seemed agreeable. The plan had just been presented and agreed to by the U.S. National Security Council.

President Cannon then stood and thanked Jon for the briefing, and said, "So now you know the seriousness of the situation. I'll expect the full cooperation from everyone here and all those you represent. We'll meet regularly to get updated briefings."

The Chairman of the Joint Chiefs of Staff then asked, "Mr. President, we're certainly on a short time string here. When will things start to move with the North Koreans in Kentucky?"

The President cupped his right hand around his right ear and said, "General, I think I can hear the cars approaching the Slusher brothers' farm as I speak."

Laughter was heard throughout the room as the NSC members stood and began chatting among themselves. The President slipped out through the back door and headed for the oval office.

Chapter 2

Pyongyang, North Korea
December 1

Kim Jong-un, North Korea's 3rd Supreme Leader, sat at his desk in one of his many palaces. Standing rigidly at attention before him was General Park Chang-Sun. Only the two of them were in the room.

Kim had a thick folder on his desk along with what remained of his breakfast. He had just polished off three steak, egg, and cheese McMuffins, four hash browns, two orders of pancakes, and two hot apple pies. Plus coffee. Kim had acquired a taste for McDonald's foods while a student in Switzerland, and after his father died and Kim became Supreme Leader he sent a contingent of his cooks to Switzerland to learn the McDonalds menu and be able to duplicate it for him in Pyongyang. The cooks stayed four weeks to accomplish this, and each gained 12 pounds. But they returned home with the ability to replicate all the McDonald menu items. Kim loved to eat, and at 5 foot 5 inches tall and 330 pounds he had developed a serious problem with gout. It was so bad that most times he used a wheel chair. Kim had ordered General Park to report to him while he was eating breakfast at his desk. The general had arrived before Kim was finished, so he was required to stand at attention before Kim for the 20 or so minutes it took to finish breakfast.

When finished Kim pushed his intercom button and heard, "Yes, Supreme Leader." Kim replied, "I'm finished..... get this mess off my desk." "Yes, Supreme Leader."

The door to Kim's office flew open and two soldiers came rushing in with plastic garbage bags in hand. They gathered all the breakfast residue and immediately left, closing the door behind them. It took less than 1 minute total to accomplish. Kim had been watching his watch. If it had taken more than 90 seconds each of the two would have been shot by Kim. He demanded efficiency.

Kim then opened the folder on his desk and looked up at General Park. "The plan seems to be complete. It damn well better be. I don't want any screw-ups this time....do you understand me General Park?"

"Yes, Supreme Leader, I'm honored to be chosen for the task. I assure you it will be accomplished just as we have it planned. General O, General Sin, and the other four soldiers in Kentucky will be eliminated."

Kim said, "I expect to get a report from you every day after you arrive in the U.S. You have a satellite cell phone and you will report your progress daily. You have until Christmas to accomplish your mission. Is that clear?"

"Yes, Supreme Leader, I understand and will report daily and will have completed my mission by Christmas," General Park replied.

Kim responded, "You are free to go. And as you pass my secretary tell her I want a large chocolate milkshake ASAP."

General Park nodded, turned, and walked out of Kim's office.

As he awaited his chocolate milkshake Kim sat back in his chair and reflected on the two American missions he had underway. Just as soon as the six soldier team failed to accomplish their mission about a year ago Kim dispatched a team of three soldiers with orders to locate the six and kill them. They failed. Kim then sent another team. Same result. Each team was executed upon their return to North Korea, and Kim then started working on the plan to deliver a nuclear bomb to Los Angeles. He completed that plan about a month ago, and it was well underway. He then started to again think about his revenge for the failed mission of the six soldiers that were now in Kentucky. After thinking about it, he decided to send just one person, his very best general, to accomplish his revenge. Both missions were now underway. Kim got a giant smile on his face just as his chocolate milkshake arrived.

———

Ishigaki Port, Japan

Captain Saito was master of the Japanese Feeder Class Container ship **Taka Maru**, owned by the OKN Line. The ship was currently docked at the South Japan port of Ishigaki. Captain Saito was on the bridge talking to his Second Officer, Kozo, "It looks like we're going to be here until toward the end of December. We've got quite a bit more work to be done before we can get underway. The overhaul of our engines has taken longer than expected. Just as soon as we can start steaming we'll head straight to Chongjin, North Korea. We've got a strange load to pick up there. We pick up only five containers, but our instructions are to make sure that all five are placed on deck such that our ship cranes can readily reach each of them. We will also take on a dozen North Koreans who will assemble the parts when they arrive in Venezuela. They also said that they may need to work on the parts during the passage, so it's important that their containers are readily accessible. Since we'll be already loaded with all our cargo other than that from North Korea, we'll be ready to set sail to Venezuela just as soon as we leave port at Chongjin. How long will that passage take?"

Kozo, typing data into his computer, said, "Captain, it's about 9000 miles from Chongjin to Venezuela. If we average about 25 knots we're looking at 13 days. Getting through the Panama Canal could delay us another day, so I'd say two weeks."

Captain Saito said, "The North Koreans want to us to leave Chongjin on January 1. So that would put us in Venezuela mid January. That timing seems to be okay with everyone. How far is the trip from here to Chongjin?"

Kozo punched in more numbers on his computer and said, "1250 miles. That will take us about 43 hours."

"To load in Chongjin should not take long at all, only five containers and the twelve North Koreans. So if we can leave here shortly after Christmas we should be good," replied the captain. "I don't have any idea what the cargo is we're picking up in Korea, but their government is paying us top dollar....so I plan to cooperate fully with their wishes."

Captain Saito then thought, *And another strange thing about this trip is that OKN Line was contacted by the Japanese government with a request that before we leave for Chongjin we accept a passenger named Cho who will serve as an engineering officer, and OKN Line ordered me to disclose nothing about Mr. Cho. He must be some kind of government observer.*

Chapter 3

Harlan County, Kentucky
December 1

It was quite a sight to behold! Ten people sitting in rocking chairs across the front porch of the Slusher brothers' magnificent country home. It looked very similar to the porch on a Cracker Barrel restaurant. All ten were lined up in a row. All were slowly rocking. Eight of the ten had cats in their laps, and were gently stroking them. A contented assembly if there ever was one!

Gunsmoke and Booger Slusher were fifty three and fifty one years old, respectively. Their real given names were James Robert and Jay Alan, but everyone always just called them by their nicknames, Gunsmoke and Booger. Gunsmoke was called that because as a kid he loved watching Matt Dillon on the television show Gunsmoke. When Jay Alan was born his mother proclaimed him "a cute little booger." So the brothers were called Gunsmoke and Booger since childhood. About 21 years ago Gunsmoke purchased a super lottery ticket on a whim (he normally never gambled or got lottery tickets) and it turned out to be the sole winner. He received a check for just over 100 million dollars. He opted to not be identified (back then you had that option), and he and Booger purchased the 50 acre plot of land they now live on and had an enormous country home built on it. The home, a huge ranch, had four bedrooms at each end, each with a private bath, and a very large living room, dining room, kitchen, two studies, and a great room in the central part of the house. Attached all around the house was a 12 foot wide porch. The brothers highly valued their privacy. The entire 50 acres were secured by a 7 foot high wire fence with barbed-wire strung along its top. Security cameras were located everywhere. One came to the Slusher farm by traveling north on highway 119 from Harlan toward the town of Cumberland. About 10 miles from Harlan there was a road on the left that wound for about a mile before coming to a gate with a gatehouse. There was a sign there that read, *"Private Property. No Trespassing, No Vendors, No Visitors without invitation."* It was the entrance to the Slusher farm. From six am to three pm a fellow named Charlie served as guard at the gate and stayed in the gatehouse. From three pm until midnight George relieved Charlie. From midnight to 6 am the gate was locked and no one was admitted. For emergencies there was an intercom that permitted conversation between the gate and the guest house where Charlie and George lived. They were both single, and had gone to high school with the Slusher brothers. One other person, also single, Ray, was employed for security. Ray patrolled the fence during daylight hours and also ran errands. He too had attended high school with the brothers and Charlie and George and stayed in the third bedroom of the guest house. No one was allowed to pass through the gate without a prior invitation from one of the brothers, with one exception. August J. "Gus" Richenberger was the brothers' financial advisor. He lived in Knoxville, Tennessee, a distance of about 100 miles from Harlan. Gus was the principal in the firm of Richenberger Financial. As soon as Gunsmoke realized he had won the lottery he started looking for an advisor. He knew he could not effectively manage 100 million dollars. He knew no one he could turn to. Very fortunately for him, he simply picked Gus Richenberger from the Knoxville yellow pages. When Gus got the phone call he immediately dropped what he was doing and drove to Harlan County to meet with the brothers. The three of them became the best of friends, and with Gus' advice he had successfully turned their 100 million into over 350 million in the 21 years since they first met. Gunsmoke and Booger agreed that hiring Gus was the smartest and luckiest move they had ever made. Gus was totally honest, hard working, smart, extremely knowledgeable about investments and also a super guy to work with. He was the only person that could drive up to the gate and be admitted by either Charlie or George without the brothers' consent. The brothers did not have many friends and very few family members. When they received their lottery money they told those that knew them that they had been very lucky with some investments and that had enabled them to purchase the large farm and home. Very little of their money was placed in the Harlan banks, at the advice of Gus Richenberger, because small town banks "had mouths and ears." Almost all their holdings were placed by Gus in firms in Knoxville, New York, and Atlanta. Thus their wealth had remained totally unknown to anyone other than the three. When friends and family inquired about such things they were simply told that their investments had really done well. So it was that Gunsmoke and Booger managed to live in Harlan County without being known to be super wealthy. They even still each drove 10 year old pick-up trucks. They did give handsomely to charities, with advice from Gus. Being devout Christians they gave 10% of their yearly earnings to worthy charities around the world, including a $250,000 annual anonymous contribution to the Loving Arms Baptist Church in Benham, Kentucky where they attended as children. Remarkably, the Slusher brothers' wealth was unknown to anyone but Gus Richenberger.

Just a little over a year ago Gunsmoke and Booger having read in the newspapers and viewed on television the news about the mysterious golden anchor crosses, the first of which had been discovered in Harlan County about 16 years ago, decided that they would like to purchase one for each of them to wear as protection from possible harm. At the Anchor Cross Festival last year all six of the anchor crosses were displayed, accompanied by their owners. So the Slusher brothers met with all the owners and asked if any two of the beautiful artifacts might be purchased. After deliberation, the owners unanimously agreed to keep possession of all the anchor crosses and allow Dr. Randy Peters to keep them at his Center in Lexington for further study and research. It was at that same festival that the six soldiers dispatched by Supreme Leader Kim Jung-un showed up in Harlan and made an attempt to steal all six of the artifacts. After their failed attempt the six were arrested by Harlan County Sheriff J. Bert Sterling. The sheriff soon came to understand that the six were just soldiers carrying out the orders of a madman, and Sheriff Sterling contacted the Slusher brothers to see if they would allow the Koreans to work on their farm until their applications for political asylum were processed. They agreed, and the six had been there ever since. The political asylum had been granted about six months ago, but all six Koreans wanted to continue to live and work for the Slusher brothers. They had been given the four bedrooms on one end of the house. Two of the six were North Korean generals, the other four were soldiers of various ranks. The two generals, O Kuk-mu and Sin Ji-hae, were each given a private bedroom. The other two bedrooms were shared by two soldiers each. It had proven to be a great arrangement.....the Koreans had developed a strong attachment for the brothers and their three security guards, and the guards and brothers had likewise gotten to understand and appreciate each of the North Koreans.

All ten continued to rock on the porch. It was about 3:30 pm on Thursday, December 1. Kentucky was experiencing an unusually warm day. The high temperature was predicted to be 60 degrees, and the skies were a beautiful dark blue with fluffy white clouds floating along. Gunsmoke said, "Sheriff, we always welcome you and Kyle to our home. We feel very fortunate to have such outstanding law enforcement officers as you two, and we'll never forget your involvement with our good North Korean friends here. If it wasn't for you I don't know what would have happened to them." Gunsmoke rocked gently and stroked the beautiful orange tabby cat in his lap.

Sheriff Sterling replied, "Well, Gunsmoke, the fact is that without the generosity of you and Booger our good Korean friends would have had a real problem. Taking them in as you did was a God-send."

"Sheriff, it worked out extremely well all the way around. They are among the finest folks I've ever met, and they work hard here at the farm and more than earn their keep. Booger and I feel very fortunate to have them, and we've truly come to appreciate and love them." Gunsmoke said.

General O Kuk-mu said, "I know I speak for all of us when I say we feel so blessed to be here, Mr. Gunsmoke. And Mr. Sheriff and Mr. Kyle are equally our friends. We all thank you so much for your help." General O stroked the large, gray cat softly purring in his lap.

Booger petted the small black and white kitten in his lap and said, "Okay, enough of all this we-like-each-other talk, what brings you two lawmen to our home today?"

Kyle Potter was the 10 year old kid who found the first anchor cross in Harlan County about 16 years ago. Now he is Sheriff Sterling's chief deputy, after receiving a degree in law enforcement from Eastern Kentucky University in Richmond, Kentucky. He is also the owner of the Seibert Anchor Cross.

Kyle said, "Booger, Gunsmoke, I'm sure Bert would agree with me when I say that I wish we were just here for a social visit, and it sure is most delightful sitting here on the porch with all of you, but we do have a little business we need to discuss. As you know, when you all applied for political asylum you were each debriefed by federal agents of the U.S. Citizenship and Immigration Services (USCIS). The information you gave them was entered into a federal database which could be accessed by other pertinent federal agencies. And, as you also know, Sheriff Sterling was questioned about you during the course of their review for your political asylum application. Bert, would you like to take it from here?"

Sheriff Sterling continued, "Sure Kyle. I got a call around noon today from a federal intelligence agent. I'm not at liberty to reveal who he was or what agency he was with, but due to a very serious pending situation the agency had come across the six of you by looking over their databases. You fit exactly the profile they were looking for. They then gave me a call and asked if I would help them by coming here to alert you to their upcoming visit. They wanted me to assure you that you were not in any trouble at all, and that your political asylum was not in question. What they need is your assistance. They cannot force you to help, but would like to come here to talk about the situation and see if you might agree to voluntarily assist them. They would not tell me the exact nature of their problem, but just wanted my office's help by seeing if you would agree to their visit. "

General Sin Ji-hae then said, "Sounds very serious, Mr. Sheriff. Are you sure we're not in some kind of trouble?"

"That I can assure you, General Sin," replied Bert. "They are only looking to see if you might be agreeable to voluntarily help them. Apparently you are in a unique position to be able to do that. That's about all I know about it. But they are in a hurry, and they said I was to call them back today to let them know your decision. If you agree, then they would be here tomorrow afternoon to have discussions with you."

General O then said, "If there's any way we can help our new country, we would want to do so." He then paused and looked at his five comrades. Each stopped rocking and petting their cats long enough to vigorously nod their heads in agreement.

Bert responded, "I thought you might say that, and I want you to know I'm really proud of you guys. I don't know what's up, but your willingness to talk with them is super. I'll make the call to them as we drive back to the office. If you would, please alert Charlie and George that they will be here sometime tomorrow afternoon, and after they have identified themselves to let them in the gate."

Gunsmoke said, "Roger that sheriff. We'll make sure they have no problem with us. Also, please tell them when you call that we have two extra bedrooms that they would be welcome to use if their schedules permitted it."

"Very, very kind of you," Bert said. "I'll pass that along to them."

Booger then said, "Okay, now that business is over how about a big glass of sweet tea?"

Kyle replied, "Yeah man, that sounds real good." Bert nodded in agreement.

Booger and Gunsmoke stood and then walked inside to get the tea. The cats that were in their laps tagged along behind them. The Koreans again started rocking and petting their cats.

The Slusher brothers had been cat lovers since they were kids. For as long as they could remember there were cats in their home. Their parents always had at least two or three. When they won the lottery and moved to their new home they brought three cats with them, and since then they frequently visited the animal shelter and always returned home with one or two new cats or kittens. Presently they had somewhere around 25 cats on their property. And they were all very well cared for.

Perhaps their very favorite cat had been Smoky. They adopted her about 16 years ago. Smoky was a beautiful gray tabby, and extremely smart. She was also very loving, playful, and curious. About a year after acquiring her as a small kitten from the shelter she wondered off the farm and into a nearby church when deliveries were being made through the back door. She was trapped in the back room when the delivery man didn't notice her as he closed and locked the door. Unfortunately, a few hours later a fire broke out in the front part of the church and when the fire fighters arrived they heard Smoky screaming at the top of her lungs from the smoke filled back room. They rescued her and took her to a vet to be examined. He proclaimed her fine other than inhaling some smoke and said she should recover without problems. The firemen inquired from the pastor of the church about ownership of the cat, but he told them he knew nothing about her. They then took her to the Harlan County Sheriff's Office. Deputy Rosie Cain immediately fell in love with the cat and begged Sheriff J. Bert Sterling to keep her in the office as a mascot. He finally agreed. Because she was found screaming in a church Rosie named her Preacher Puss. She adapted well to the sheriff's office, and all the employees and visitors loved her.

Soon after being adopted by Rosie it was found that Preacher Puss had a very unusual sensitivity.....she hated guns! This was discovered when a deputy pulled his pistol to clean it. Preacher Puss had been given a shelf above and to the side of the front door. She slept there, and could be found there most of the time napping or just watching what was going on in the sheriff's office. The deputy's desk was directly below the cat's shelf. When he pulled his gun for cleaning Preacher Puss immediately jumped from her loft with all four feet and claws extended and landed directly atop the deputy's arm. The gun fell to the floor, the deputy screamed in agony with blood streaming down his arm. Preacher Puss then calmly retracted her claws and jumped back to her shelf. Preacher Puss had just established that drawn guns would not be tolerated in the sheriff's department! Many instances after that occurred where bad guys had drawn weapons in the office only to be subdued by Preacher Puss. She quickly gained a reputation as one of the department's most effective members.

The Slusher brothers were unable to locate their Smoky, and after searching every day for about a week finally gave up the search. They were heartbroken. And then a strange thing happened. When the North Koreans were captured by Sheriff Sterling a little over a year ago they were held temporarily in the sheriff's holding cell. After Bert had contacted the Slusher brothers to see if they would agree to employ the Koreans and they agreed, the brothers came to the sheriff's department to meet the Koreans. When that happened, Smoky, aka Preacher Puss, was found playing with the Koreans. When the brothers saw the cat they immediately recognized her, and she them, and there was a great reunion. After hearing the Preacher Puss story from Rosie, the brothers agreed to leave the cat in the sheriff's department. She was too loved and too important there to be moved. Everyone was greatly pleased with the arrangement.....especially Preacher Puss! The brothers frequently dropped by to see and spend time with the cat.

Gunsmoke and Booger had promised each of the six Koreans that they would be given a cat when they moved to the Slusher farm. So soon after arriving there each of the six adopted one of the many cats. It was a great therapy for them. Indeed cats were a prominent and very important element at the Slusher farm.

The front door flew open and Gunsmoke, Booger, and two cats came back onto the front porch. The brothers each had a tray that contained 5 huge glasses of sweet tea. After they were distributed all took their seats.

Deputy Kyle Potter said, "Guys, how could it get any better than this? Here we sit on a gorgeous December day with good friends rocking and drinking sweet tea!" All nodded in agreement.

After finishing their tea and spinning a few more tall tales Bert said, "It's been most enjoyable, and I sure do appreciate the cooperation you've all shown for the upcoming feds visit tomorrow. Kyle and I will take off now. Please keep us informed about everything."

All stood and shook hands. Gunsmoke said, "We sure will. Soon as we get settled with our visitors tomorrow I'll give you a call. As always, we sure enjoyed your visit. Come back anytime."

Kyle reached down and petted the cat standing at his feet. Bert did likewise, and then the two got in their cruiser and headed back toward town.

Chapter 4

Pyongyang, North Korea
December 15

General Park Chang-Sun sat alone in his apartment. He stared at the packed suitcases sitting on his bed. His official car and driver would be arriving in about 15 minutes to take him to the airport. He would fly from Pyongyang to Toyko, and then after a two hour layover he would fly to Knoxville, Tennessee in the United States, with stops along the way in Los Angeles, California and Atlanta, Georgia. Upon arriving in Knoxville he would be met by a person with the unusual name of Pretty Boy Maggard. Maggard would identify himself by holding a sign in the area of baggage claim that said *"Mr. Chang"*.

General Park reached in his suit's breast pocket and pulled out his newly acquired passport. It was a Chinese document that had his picture with a name of Mr. Wong Chang. The

North Korean intelligence people had produced a flawless fake ID. Ho knew he would have no problem with it. They had also put together a story for him that he had studied carefully now for over a week. His new identity came with a complete background of where he was born in China, his parents names, the schools he attended, names of close friends, and a complete job history. He had worked for several related companies, but was now an engineer with Zhao Electronics, a computer hardware and software company.

General Park, aka Wong Chang, then pulled the credit card from his wallet. He examined it carefully. It was a Visa credit card issued by a Chinese bank that was controlled totally by the North Korean government. The card was perfectly valid, and should work anywhere in the U.S. He then checked the currency in the wallet and counted two thousand United States dollars. He knew that once he made contact with Mr. Maggard in Knoxville he would receive a suitcase full of U.S. dollars that he might need for his mission.

Finding Mr. Maggard was a real stroke of good fortune, General Park thought. Once the Supreme Leader had contacted their intelligence people and demanded that they put everything together that was asked by him, Park knew he would be able to make the required contact. The report they generated at his request said that this Mr. Maggard, presently living in Knoxville, Tennessee, had previously been the owner of a small grocery store in Harlan County, Kentucky. It was thought that the six North Korean soldiers targeted by Park now lived somewhere in Harlan County. Maggard's Grocery was just a front for a lot of illegal activity previously conducted by Mr. Maggard from his office in the back of the store. About 16 years ago the Harlan County sheriff discovered that Maggard had millions of illegal dollars stored in lock boxes in a Harlan, Kentucky bank. Fortunately for him, he was able to escape to Columbia, South America, where he pitched in with a group of drug smugglers. He deeded over Maggard's Grocery to his friend Trigger Green who continued it's illegal operations. After several years Maggard eventually moved back to Knoxville, Tennessee where he now lives and continues working with the Columbian drug smugglers and doing any other activity that might make him money. The North Koreans had contacts with the Columbian smugglers, and through them were able to locate Mr. Maggard. With his prior Harlan contacts he seemed a perfect fit to help General Park accomplish his mission. The North Korean government sent a message via the Columbian group that they would pay Mr. Maggard 100,000 U.S. dollars to assist Mr. Chang. Pretty Boy Maggard readily agreed. The North Koreans then arranged for a transfer of $100,000 for Mr. Maggard's fee, and also for another $200,000 to be placed in a suitcase and given to Mr. Chang upon his Knoxville arrival. Mr. Maggard was instructed to take Mr. Chang to his home in Knoxville and allow him to rest there for a couple of days prior to leaving for Harlan County. Mr. Maggard was also instructed to get Mr. Chang a rental car and give him detailed instructions on how to get to Maggard's Grocery along with a letter of introduction to Trigger Green. For $100,00 Pretty Boy Maggard was delighted to comply.

There was a sharp knock on General Park's door. The driver was here. His trip had begun.

Kim Jung-un rocked back in his chair and put his gout plagued feet up on his desk. It was mid-afternoon and the Supreme Leader had just finished a snack. He felt much better after eating three cheeseburgers, two orders of fries, and a large chocolate milkshake. He reflected on the plans currently underway for the U.S.

General Park had just left on his trip. Everything was all set for taking out the six traitors that had failed their mission and then elected to remain in the United States rather than to return home and face the consequences. On reflection, he couldn't really blame them, since he'd have had them executed the moment they returned.....and they knew it. Justice must now be rendered. They must die, and General Park would accomplish the mission. When he does, I'll reward him with another star, Kim thought.

His thoughts then turned to the pending nuclear attack. Twelve of his finest naval personnel had been chosen for this mission. The ranking officer, Admiral Sung Ho-Jun, was one of Kim's favorites. Sung was 48 years old and extremely well versed in all the aspects of the nuclear launch. He had served approximately 5 years with the nuclear program, and knew everything about how to arm and launch the missile. Sung was also an extremely fine physical specimen. He would take the lead in the mission. The other officer was Lieutenant Commander Shin In-Tak. Shin had less service than Sung, but was also trained in all aspects of a nuclear launch as well as seamanship. That, plus the fact that the two and been good friends and had worked together for the past 8 years made them a perfect choice. The other ten assigned to the mission were NCOs, one Chief Petty Officer, one Petty Officer First Class, and eight Able Seamen. All twelve had been training for a mission such as this for about 3 years. They knew how to accomplish launching a missile with a nuclear warhead at sea from a mobile launcher

The team was already at the North Korean port of Chongjin. They had acquired a storage building immediately adjacent to the slip where the **Taka Maru** would be told to tie up to take on the five containers and 12 member North Korean team. In four of those containers were all the equipment required to launch the missile. In the fifth container, one specially marked with red letters saying *"Use Extreme Caution"*, was the nuclear warhead along with some additional needed equipment and parts. The team and all the containers had arrived at Chongjin two days ago. The team was staying in the storage building, guarding the containers. The arrival of the **Taka Maru** was still about two weeks out, but the team would use that time to rehearse their mission to be at peak readiness by the end of the month.

The pain shooting up his legs from his gout-diseased feet would normally have caused Kim to wince, but the anticipated nuclear attack on the United States was enough to cause a huge smile to form on his face instead. They won't know what hit them, he thought. After that attack I'll contact the White House and present them with facts that will establish beyond any doubt that we did it, and then I'll deliver my list of demands that they must meet. If they refuse, then I'll threaten them with similar attacks on New York, Washington, Miami, and San Francisco. North Korea will then be recognized as THE major world power. Riches and power will follow beyond my wildest expectations! The pain from his gout could no longer be felt! What a great birthday present awaited him on January 8th.

Chapter 5

Harlan County, Kentucky
December 16

Fatso Chapel stopped his car, stuck his head out the window and yelled, "Hey Charlie, Gunsmoke called and asked me to come over."

Fatso worked for Trigger Green at Maggard's Grocery. Even though Trigger was mostly engaged in illegal activities, he and Harlan County Sheriff J. Bert Sterling had a very healthy respect for each other. On several occasions Trigger had leaked information to the sheriff that had saved his life. Trigger actually liked Bert, and would not do or be associated with anything to knowingly hurt him. The sheriff, while always vigilant to find illegal activity going on at Maggards, appreciated Trigger and his assistance on those occasions where human life could be in danger. Bert knew very well that Trigger was involved in selling stolen goods, credit card fraud, moonshine, robberies, making book, etc., but was seldom able to catch him at it. Trigger was very good at what he did. Fatso Chapel worked the grocery store for Trigger. He stocked the groceries, and could normally be found at the cash register sitting in a chair watching a small television or reading a book. There was also another screen below the counter that was hooked up to several security cameras that scanned the outside parking lot, the back of the store, a couple inside the grocery store, and one in Trigger's office, located through a door at the back of the grocery. There was also a button beside the security monitor that opened the lock on the door going into Trigger's office. No one got in to see Trigger without first going through Fatso. And going through Fatso could sometimes be a pain.....he just loved to tell corny jokes. Everyone who knew Fatso was well aware that he loved to tell his jokes, and many tried to avoid him because of it.

"Hey Fatso," replied Charlie from the Slusher Brothers' guardhouse, "go right on in, the brothers are expecting you." Charlie pressed the button to raise the gate from across the road.

The gate slowly started to rise.

"Thanks Charlie, but before I go you gotta tell me how you get out of an elephant's stomach."

Charlie looked peeved and said, "How the hell would I know?"

Fatso replied, "You get out of an elephant's stomach by running around until you're pooped out."

Charlie grinned, shook his head, and waved at Fatso as he pulled through the gate.

Fatso continued on the road to the Slusher Brothers' country home. It came into view after driving another quarter mile. Fatso always marveled at the magnificent structure. He thought, *Ole Gunsmoke and Booger sure know how to make good investments.*

"How you doing, Fatso," Gunsmoke shouted as Fatso parked his car in front of the home and started out the opened door.

"Good Morning Gunsmoke," replied Fatso. "Doing okay as far as I know. You boys doing well?" He walked up onto the front porch and sat down in a rocking chair beside Gunsmoke and Booger. The sun was shining brightly, but the temperature was a cool 40 degrees. All were wearing warm clothes and jackets.

Booger replied, "Still going. Doctors ain't told us no different. Who's minding the store while you're gone"

"Cousin Whalebait's looking after it for me," Fatso replied. "You boys know why an elephant puts skates on before he goes to bed?"

Gunsmoke and Booger just stared blankly at Fatso.

"So he can get rolling in the morning," Fatso chuckled.

Gunsmoke then said, "Okay, enough of that. I got some business I want to discuss with you."

"Sure thing, Gunsmoke," Fatso said. "Where are my good Korean friends?"

"They're all working," replied Booger. "I'll round them up to come see you before you leave, but first we got business, like Gunsmoke said."

Fatso had become very close friends with the six North

Koreans. He had first met them when he was directed by Trigger to drive them from Maggard's Grocery into Harlan for the ACFes about 14 months ago. They loved his corny jokes. After they were placed at the Slusher farm Fatso would come out at least once a week to visit and tell them more of his jokes. They never seemed not to enjoy them. They were true friends.

"Okay," said Fatso. "So what's the business we need to talk about?"

Gunsmoke replied, "Well, if my math is correct 9 days from today is Christmas. It comes on Sunday this year, and everyone here at the farm will be in church for much of the day. I remember last Christmas seemed a little drab here with our good Korean friends, so I wanted to do something special this year. What I had in mind was a little Christmas Eve party here at the farm. We'll invite several folks from town to join us for a big dinner and then a special present opening. I've been told by several town people that you have been known to play Santa Claus. Your robust size would lend itself well for doing that. So I was hoping I could hire you to come to our dinner, and then after we finish with the meal to slip out and get all dressed up in a Santa suit and then come in with a big 'Ho, Ho, Ho' and distribute gifts to everyone from the huge bag you'll be carrying over your shoulder. What'd you say?"

"I say I'd be pleased as punch to do that, and I'll do it for free," replied Fatso. "Course I'd expect a good meal and maybe even a little gift to me in my bag."

"You got a deal, Fatso," proclaimed Booger. "We'll make sure you get double portions on all the food and we'll have a nice gift for you. Can you be here around 6 on Christmas Eve? We'll serve dinner at 7 and you'll need to get all your gear arranged."

"Not a problem," said Fatso. "I'll be here at 6 with bells on." He said with a smile on his face. "Who's in charge of getting all the gifts?"

Gunsmoke said, "I'll make a list and give it to Ray to go into town and pick up the gifts and get each of them wrapped. I want to get some really special nice watches for the Koreans, and I'll send Ray to Diamondcraft Jewelry to pick those up. Most of the other gifts he can probably find at Wal-Mart. We'll have them here in your bag ready to distribute on Christmas Eve. Also, I've commissioned Mrs. Cavanaugh to make you a custom Santa suit. She'll drop by Maggards and measure you up for it. She said she'd try and get by tomorrow. You be looking for her. She said she could have it ready for you by the middle of next week"

One of the Slusher cats jumped up in Fatso's lap. He started stroking the cat, who responded by starting his motor and swishing his tail. As Fatso petted him Gunsmoke said, "You stay right here and talk with Booger and pet that cat. I'm going in to round up the gang to come visit with you a bit before you get gone." Gunsmoke walked into the house.

Three or four minutes later there was a loud commotion coming from inside the home, and then the six Koreans came bounding out onto the front porch with big grins on their face. They all shook hands with Fatso and slapped him on his back. Fatso did not stand, being careful not to disturb the cat enjoying his lap. All six took a seat on the porch in front of Fatso and they talked for several minutes. General O then said, "Mr. Fatso, before you leave you've got to tell us a joke."

"Sure," said Fatso. "You know why elephants are such poor dancers?"

The Koreans looked at each other with wide eyes and big grins, and then turned and looked directly at Fatso, slowly shaking their heads.

"Elephants are poor dancers because they have two left feet!" proclaimed Fatso.

The Koreans then started to roll around on the floor of the porch laughing. They finally composed themselves, stood up, and each shook hands with Fatso as they went back to work.

Fatso finally set the cat down gently on the floor and stood. He said to the brothers, "I sure thank you boys for thinking of me and inviting me to play Santa. I know I'll really enjoy it. I'll look for Mrs. Cavanaugh tomorrow, and will then plan to see you at 6 pm on Christmas Eve."

Gunsmoke replied, "We thank you Fatso. It'll be a great evening. See you then."

Fatso then walked to his car, got in and started the engine, and then honked a couple of times as he drove off. Gunsmoke and Booger waved.

The brothers continued rocking and petting their cats. After a few minutes Booger said, "It sure has been interesting around here lately.....since those intelligence people showed up."

"It has been that," replied Gunsmoke. "It would seem all is going well with them, but of course we don't know everything that's going on."

The brothers then fell silent, continued rocking, and reflected on what had happened since the feds arrived.

———

On December 2nd, the afternoon after Sheriff Sterling and Deputy Potter's visit giving them a 'heads-up' regarding the upcoming arrival of federal intelligence agents that had business with the Koreans, two ladies dressed in neat dark suits arrived at the gate driving a dark colored sedan. They identified themselves to Charlie as Agents Clair Eaton and Rose McKay. They each flipped open their credentials pack for him to see. Charlie then phoned the brothers, and was told to allow the feds to enter and proceed to their home.

"Thank you ladies," Charlie said as he pressed the button to raise the gate. "Please drive on in to the home......you can't miss it!"

Agent Eaton replied, "Thank you."

The agents had been dispatched by CIA Director Kennan to meet with the Koreans to determine which of them might be best suited for the task of joining the crew of *Taka Maru* for the purpose of preventing the launch of the nuclear missile. The agents had been thoroughly briefed, and were well aware of the extremely serious nature of the mission. Specifically, they were to accomplish two goals. The first was to establish if any one of the six seemed best suited to carry out the dangerous task. If that was found to be the case, then their second goal was to train the selected person to assume the identity of Mr. Cho and to establish several scenarios whereby he would be able to stop the missile launch. One problem that faced Director Kennan was whether only one person should or could do the job. Maybe two or more would be required. So he decided that they would proceed with their planning under the assumption that the agents would be able to find one of the Koreans suitable. If that was not the case then they would have to adjust the plans. Accordingly, Director Kennan had contacted his counterpart in the Japanese government and told him that the U.S. had a very serious situation developing, and requested their assistance in placing Mr. Cho aboard the ***Taka Maru***. The original intelligence about the planned nuclear strike had come to the CIA from sources within North Korea, so the Japanese knew nothing about what was taking place. They simply received the request from Director Kennan regarding Mr. Cho and complied with his wishes. All of this took place around the middle of November, about one month ago.

The brothers watched the black sedan approaching their home. Gunsmoke said, "Booger, that sure looks like a government car."

Booger said, "Yep, I could spot it a mile off."

The agents arrived, and after introductions with the brothers the four took seats on the front porch. Clair Eaton then said, "Gentlemen, Agent McKay and myself greatly appreciate your cooperation in this matter. I know you realize how serious it is. Let me also thank you for the invitation to stay here in your lovely home, but Rose and I have motel rooms in Harlan. Regulations, you understand. Our plans are to come here each afternoon to accomplish our work with the Koreans. We'll try and interfere as little as possible with their work for you, but it will be necessary, with your agreement, that we be able to interview each of them. Is that okay?"

Gunsmoke looked at Booger and said, "Well, I guess so. Sheriff Sterling explained to us that this was something very important to our country, so we certainly want to help anyway we can."

"Great," Agent Eaton said. "We certainly thank you for your assistance."

With that the agents had been coming to the Slusher farm every day since December 2nd. They had quickly discovered that General O Kuk-mu and General Sin Ji-hae were the natural leaders of the group. Then, after several days of interviewing the two generals it was determined that General O seemed to possess all the attributes required for the mission. The agents then contacted Director Kennan saying that they recommended General O as the sole person to accomplish stopping the nuclear attack. They told Kennan that General O had actually started in the North Korean military in the navy, and had served almost ten years assigned to one of their guided-missile patrol boats. He had then been singled out for advancement, and was transferred to serve in the army. He had several years of experience in their nuclear program, and was familiar with all aspects of it. He had quickly risen in the ranks, and had achieved the rank of General by the time he was 42 years old. Kim Jung-un had selected him to lead the team of six on the mission to the United States because of his excellent service record. Thus his background was ideally suitable to go on the mission to defeat the pending nuclear strike. In addition to his experience, his personality was deemed perfect to accept responsibility for the mission, and he seemed anxious to accomplish it. Director Kennan agreed. General O was the man for the mission!

The agents had been very careful in their interviews with the six Koreans to not divulge the exact nature of the mission. They wanted only the person selected to know that it involved stopping a threatened nuclear strike against the U.S. So other than the two federal agents, only General O knew about the planned strike, and he had been instructed to keep that information strictly to himself.

———

Booger stroked the cat in his lap and said, "Brother, I sure hope Mrs. Cavanaugh has plenty of cloth to make Fatso's Santa outfit. That ole boy looked like he'd gained another 50 pounds."

"Now, now Booger," Gunsmoke replied, "you shouldn't be talking about somebody's weight. Fatso is a large person, and that's exactly what we need for our Santa."

Booger said, "I didn't mean anything by it. Just an observation. And you are right, he will make us a real good Santa Claus."

Ryu Jae-gyu came through the front door and said to the brothers, "Gentlemen, lunch is served. Please come to the dining room."

Ryu had assumed the cooking duties since the six Koreans came to the Slusher farm. He had always enjoyed cooking, and now he delighted in planning and cooking for the eight of them.

Gunsmoke and Booger both gently placed their cats on the floor, stood, and started walking in the house for lunch.

Chapter 6

Harlan County, Kentucky
December 17

Your name is what?" asked Fatso as he looked at the oriental gentleman standing before him at the check-out counter.

"My name Wong Chang," the stranger repeated for Fatso. "And I here to see Mr. Trigger Green."

"What kind of a name is that?" asked Fatso. "You got the Wong name?"

"That is my name. Please, I would like to speak with Mr. Trigger Green," repeated Mr. Chang.

"I might be able to arrange that," Fatso said. "But first, you know what the hotel manager said to the elephant who couldn't pay his bill?"

Mr. Chang stared blankly.

Fatso answered with a chuckle, "He said pack your trunk and get out!"

Mr. Chang stared blankly.

Fatso shook his head, pressed the intercom button to Trigger's office, and said, "Hey Trigger, there's a Mr. Wong Chang here to see you".

A voice came back over the intercom, "Yes, please send him in."

Fatso pressed the button to release the lock on the door to Trigger's office. He then pointed toward the back of the store and said, "Right through that door back there."

"Thank you," replied Mr. Chang as he started walking toward Trigger's office.

As Mr. Chang, aka General Park Chang-Sun, entered Trigger's office he was met by an outstretched hand. The two shook hands and then Trigger said, "Please, Mr. Chang, do have a seat." Trigger walked back behind his desk and sat. Mr. Chang was seated in front of Trigger's desk.

Trigger then said, "Mr. Maggard phoned me and said you would be visiting here in Harlan County. He said that perhaps I might be of service to you. I really don't know much more than that."

Mr. Chang replied, "Thank you for seeing me Mr. Green. Yes, Mr. Maggard was quite helpful, and he said you could likely be of great assistance to me. He also said I could share information with you in confidence. Is that true?"

Trigger nodded affirmatively and said, "Yes, if you employ my services I will certainly keep our relationship just between us."

"I'm prepared to offer you $25,000 for assistance. I will only be here in Harlan for a week or so," Mr. Chang said.

"How do you think I might help you," asked Trigger.

"Do we have an agreement?" asked Mr. Chang.

"Yes, I think we do, based on the money you're offering and that you were recommended by Mr. Maggard," replied Trigger as he reached across his desk to shake hands with his new client.

"Thank you," Mr. Chang said as he shook hands with Trigger. "To everyone here in Harlan County that I meet I will say that I'm a computer hardware and software engineer from China with the firm of Zhao Electronics. I'm here to evaluate whether this county might be suitable for my firm to build a small manufacturing facility to produce computer parts and software. That, however, is not true. My real purpose in being here is to make contact with one of the North Koreans caught last year trying to steal the golden artifacts during your festival held in Harlan. The person I'm looking for is Mr. Choe Yong-ho. I represent Choe's family, and they have hired me to bring him back home."

"I see," Trigger said. "So you're going to kidnap him?"

Chang replied, "Yes, I believe that is the term you use. I am aware that he along with the other five soldiers applied for political asylum and were granted such. So I must assume that Choe is satisfied with his life here in the U.S. But his family thinks he has been....I think the term you use is, brainwashed. At any rate, his family is quite wealthy and they have hired me to bring him back home. If that involves drugging him, or bringing him against his will, then I'm prepared to do that."

"I see," said Trigger. "So what is it you want me to do?"

"Just assist me in locating him, and help me during my stay here. I only want information from you. I'm not asking you to be involved in the kidnapping."

"Good, because if you were I was going to decline your generous offer," replied Trigger.

Mr. Chang then reached into his pocket and produced an envelope and handed it to Trigger. When Trigger opened it he found a bundle of one hundred dollar bills.

Mr. Chang said, "You will find that to be $15,000. I'll pay you the other $10,000 before I leave with Choe."

Trigger grinned and said, "That is acceptable." He put the money back in the envelope and placed it in his desk.

Mr. Chang then said, "So what I need right now is a motel room and any information you might have about Choe's location."

Trigger picked up the intercom and said, "Hey Fatso, call up at Mountain Lair and get Mr. Wong Chang a room. Tell them he'll be staying there for about a week."

Trigger then said, "Okay. You got the room, now here's what I know about the six Koreans. Sheriff J. Bert Sterling got them placed at a large farm about 10 miles up highway 119 from Harlan. The farm is owned by the Slusher Brothers. It's about 50 acres, and has good security. There's a wire fence all around with barbed-wire on the top, and lots of security cameras. The brothers have three good security guards. You can't get past the gate without the approval of one of the brothers. The Koreans seldom come out of the farm."

"I understand," Mr. Chang said. "Any other information that might be useful?"

"Not really," replied Trigger. "I've never been to the farm myself, but Fatso goes there often. He's friends with the Koreans and they enjoy his visits."

Mr. Chang stood and stretched out his hand to Trigger. As they shook hands he said, "I appreciate the information. I'll get directions to the Mountain Lair from Mr. Fatso on my way out. I'll be in contact with you again before long."

"Yes," Trigger replied. "I'll look forward to hearing from you and to getting the other $10,000. Good luck."

Mr. Chang walked back to the check-out counter where Fatso was reading a book.

Fatso looked up and said, "Got your reservation. Just tell them your name when you get there. You need directions?"

"Yes," replied Mr. Chang. "Also, I understand that you are friends with the six Koreans that stay at the Slusher farm.

"Oh yeah, I sure am. They're great people," Fatso replied. "You know them?"

"Not really," Mr. Chang said. "One of my friends back home knows one of the men there, and when he heard I was going to be in this area he asked if I would personally deliver a gift to his friend. It's suppose to be a surprise, so please don't mention it."

"My lips are sealed," Fatso said. "They just invited me yesterday to come to their farm on Christmas eve to play Santa Claus. I'm going to go over and have dinner and then get all dressed up in a Santa suit and distribute gifts to everyone. It should be a fun time."

"That's nice," said Mr. Chang. "Could you now direct me to the motel?"

"Sure," Fatso said, "but first you gotta tell me what's big and grey with horns."

Mr. Chang looked puzzled.

"An elephant marching band," replied Fatso with a chuckle. He then wrote down the motel directions and went over them with Mr. Chang.

Fatso watched through the store front window as Mr. Chang drove off toward Harlan. He thought, *that man with the Wong name sure is a strange one*!

As he drove toward the motel in Harlan Mr. Chang thought, *that information I just got from Mr. Green and Mr. Fatso was just exactly what I needed. I now know the location of all six of the deserters, I know they will all be together on Christmas Eve, and I know that Mr. Fatso will be delivering a bag of presents for them to open. I think I can put together a good story to get him to slip my personal present into his bag, and when it's opened..... B O O M !! All the deserters, along with a few other unfortunate souls, will be history. And my Christmas present will be a return flight back to Pyongyang and another star from my Supreme Leader. This has been a very good day!*

Chapter 7

Harlan County, Kentucky
December 20

Badass Brown lived in a small trailer near the community of Cawood, about 8 miles south of Harlan on highway 421. Just about a quarter mile from his trailer was the home of Eagle Eye Looney. Eagle Eye and Badass were friends. Both were crooks, always into something illegal. A couple of years ago Pretty Boy Maggard drove from Knoxville, Tennessee to visit with Eagle Eye. Pretty Boy was still upset at Sheriff Sterling for discovering and confiscating 2.5 million dollars in drug money he had stored in lock boxes in a Harlan bank. He gave Eagle Eye $10,000 to kill Sheriff Sterling. Eagle Eye executed several plots to kill the sheriff, but they all failed. The last attempt was about 14 months ago at Harlan's second annual Anchor Cross Festival, ACFesII. He concocted a scheme with Badass Brown that didn't go as planned. Eagle

Eye quickly exited the county, but Badass suffered injuries and was hospitalized for several months. Ever since getting out of the hospital he had wanted to get even with the sheriff.

Bennie Sekao is one of the town drunks. Not very bright and almost always intoxicated, he roams the streets of Harlan looking for a handout so he can purchase his next bottle of booze. Normally harmless, he was tolerated by town folks and law enforcement officials. Badass Brown had driven into town and picked up Bennie and brought him back to his trailer to talk. The two sat in rickety chairs at Badass's kitchen table.

Badass said, "Bennie, it's early in the day so I'm assuming you're sober enough to talk and understand what I'm going to say to you."

"Yes sir, Badass," replied Bennie, "I'm sober as can be. Exactly what did you want to talk about?"

Badass continued, "Well, I know you remember a little over a year ago when we tried to steal those golden anchor cross things. To get everyone's attention and provide a diversion you mooned the people standing in line to view the things and then I was going to operate my contraption that would then allow me to steal them. Course it didn't work, and ole Eagle Eye got out of Dodge and I got laid up in the hospital for several months. Well, ever since then I've been trying to figure some way to get even with that damn sheriff. I've got a plan, but I need your help to carry it out."

Bennie said, "The last few plans you've cooked up haven't turned out so well. Sheriff Sterling is plenty smart. I don't know if I want to be involved again. Why would I?"

"Now, now, Bennie, don't go jumping out before you hear what I've got in mind."

"Well, I'm always open-minded," Bennie said with a grin.

"Here's what I plan to do," replied Badass. "It's almost Christmas, so I want to deliver a little Christmas gift to our sheriff. I've been working on it, and it'll be ready by Saturday, Christmas eve. I know Bert will be in his office that morning because they're shutting down for the holiday at noon. I will have a special gift box ready for you to present to the sheriff. The box will look just like a wrapped gift when he sees you holding it out for him to take. But the back side of the gift will be open, and they'll be a squirt gun inside the gift box. When Bert reaches for his gift you'll grab the box with your left hand and pull the squirt gun out with your right hand. You'll then aim the gun right at Bert's eyes and squirt them real good and shout, 'Christmas gift!'. Then you just turn and run out the door."

Bennie said, "That's crazy. Why would I do that?"

"Your reward," Badass replied, "will be I'll give you $50 plus a gallon of Trigger Green's best moonshine. How'll that be for a good Christmas gift to you?"

"Well, that part sounds pretty good. You sure all I got to do is squirt Bert in the face with water?" asked Bennie.

"That's all," said Badass. "That and shout 'Christmas gift'. That'll give me a lot of satisfaction for all the problems Bert has caused me. And it won't hurt a thing....just a little water in the face. Just a big joke."

Bennie said, "Well, I guess that would be okay. I could sure use the fifty bucks, and the moonshine would sure put me in a happy holiday mood. How do we go about this?"

Badass said, "I'll have the fake present and the squirt gun all ready to go by Saturday morning. I'll meet you in front of the court house at 9 am. Since that will be Christmas Eve, parking there should not be a problem. You just look for my old beat-up bread truck and then come to the back and knock on the door. I'll let you in and then I'll give you the fake present and squirt gun. We'll practice a couple of times and then you can make the delivery. I'll wait, and when you come running out of the sheriff's office you come back to my van and jump in and we'll take off. I'll then give you the $50 and moonshine. That sound okay?"

"Hey Badass, that sounds like it might work!" replied Bennie.

"It will," said Badass. "You just be real sure you show up at 9 on Saturday morning. You got that?"

"Got it," Bennie said.

"Great," Badass replied. "So let's have a beer to celebrate, and then I'll drive you back to town."

As Badass walked to the refrigerator to get the beers he thought, *This is going to work. I'm going to get my revenge at last. All I got to do is put together the little gift. I've already got the special squirt gun.....made entirely of materials that are not attacked by sulfuric acid.*

Chapter 8

Harlan, Kentucky
December 21

Sheriff J. Bert Sterling, Chief Deputy Kyle Potter, and pastor of the New Hope Baptist Church, Raymond Bell, sat with Mayor Fred Knapp at a table in Creech Cafe, which was located directly across the street from the Harlan County Court House that housed the Sheriff's Department. Mayor Knapp owned Creech Cafe, having inherited it from his father. The cafe was a very popular gathering spot in Harlan. School kids came in each day after school, and many old timers gathered there in the mornings to have breakfast, drink coffee, discuss the news and spin all kinds of tales. The food was super, the service great, and Fred Knapp just loved to talk with his patrons. Creech's had a couple of very unusual features. Entering through the front door you were usually greeted by a large green parrot that perched above the door. The bird's name was Polly. She had quite a vocabulary. Fred had owned Polly for many years....so many that he had lost track. In addition to greeting those entering the cafe, she loved to mooch food. There was a time many years ago when someone objected to a parrot's presence in the food establishment. However at the court hearing about half the town turned out in support of Polly, so that had not been an issue lately. The second unique feature of the cafe was the postings on all the walls. Fred loved to find interesting stories in the **Harlan Daily Enterprise**, other newspapers, and magazines. Those he deemed interesting enough he would cut out and tape up on one of the walls. He did the same with photographs. The walls were almost completely covered with such photos and articles. Whenever one of his patrons would inquire about one, Fred would take great joy in explaining in detail the story behind it. Creech Cafe was a legend in Harlan.

Sheriff Sterling said, "Guys, it's only four days until Christmas. Does everyone have their shopping all finished?"

"Got three more days to do that," Fred replied. "I don't like to get in a big hurry!" Everyone chuckled.

Pastor Bell said, "I know that each of you received an invitation to the Slusher Brothers' Christmas party Saturday evening. That should be real nice. Betty and I are looking forward to attending."

"Yes sir," the sheriff said, "I can't wait. It's not often that those boys have a party and invite townspeople. Carolyn and I are going together." Carolyn Potter was Kyle's mother. She worked as a teller at the Miner's Bank in Harlan. Carolyn and Bert had dated for years.

"Yeah, I know mom's looking forward to it. She even bought a new dress to wear," Kyle said. "I know the invitation said that we were to bring no gifts, but it sure seems funny to go to a Christmas party and not take a gift."

Fred replied, "I had the same thought, but then you know how wealthy those Slusher brothers are. I guess they just wanted our company, and I heard through the grapevine that they will have gifts for everyone."

"Whoa," Pastor Bell said. "That set 'em back some bucks."

"They can afford it," replied Fred. "I bet they got more money than anyone in Harlan County. But they're really good folks. I like them a lot."

Kyle then asked, "Hey Fred, where did you hear about the gifts....if I'm not being too nosy?"

Fred replied, "I was shopping up at DiamondCraft yesterday and saw Penny busy wrapping a whole bunch of presents.....looked mostly like very nice watches. I asked her who all the gifts were for, and she said the Slusher Brothers had sent Ray down to pick them out and that she was wrapping them for a party they were having on Saturday."

Bert was just about to take the last bite from a doughnut when Polly flew over and landed on his shoulder. Polly squawked, "Polly want a cracker, Polly want a cracker." Bert looked up at the bird and said, "No, you don't want a cracker, Polly, you want the last bite of my doughnut!" He extended it up to her. She gobbled it down.

"Polly say thank you. Polly say thank you," the bird squawked.

"You're welcome Polly," the sheriff replied. The bird flew back to her perch.

A loud cackle was heard from the back of the cafe. Fred turned and looked in that direction, and then said, "It's Mrs. Montgomery. She just read my latest posting." Fred stood and walked back to her.

"Hi Mrs. Montgomery," Fred said. "I see you saw the story about the media."

Mrs. Montgomery was still laughing. Finally she said, "Fred, that's one of your best ones. Everyone should read it."

Bert, Kyle, and Raymond then walked up and started reading the story, which said:

A man was riding his bike at the Cincinnati zoo when he saw a little girl lean into the lion's cage. Suddenly the lion grabs her by the neck of her jacket and tries to pull her into his cage. The little girl's parents are screaming. The man jumps off his bike, runs to the lion's cage, and hits the lion square on the nose with a powerful punch. The lion releases the little girl, and the man brings her to her terrified parents. They thank him profusely.

A reporter had witnessed the entire event. He said to the man, "Sir, that was the most gallant and brave thing I've seen a person do in my entire life." The man says, "Why, it was nothing, really. The lion was behind bars. I just saw this little girl in danger and acted."

The reporter said, "Well, I'll make sure this won't go unnoticed. I'm a journalist, and tomorrow's paper will have this story on the front page. So, tell me, what do you do for a living and what political affiliations do you have?

The man says, "I'm a U.S. Marine and a Republican."

The journalist leaves.

The following morning the man buys a paper out of curiosity to see if it indeed brings news of his actions, and reads, on the front page:

U.S. Marine Assaults African Immigrant and Steals His Lunch!

That pretty much sums up the media's approach to news these days.

The three men giggle and then turn to leave. Bert says to Fred, "Mr. Mayor, you sure do have good wallpaper." Kyle and Raymond nod in agreement.

Chapter 9

Mrs. Cavanaugh said, "Fatso, you quit that wiggling. How can I tell if the Santa suit fits if you can't stand still?" Mrs. Cavanaugh was standing behind the grocery store's checkout counter trying to make sure that the new Santa outfit she made for Fatso fit properly. Fatso stood beside her wearing the new bright red and white outfit.

"Mrs. Cavanaugh, do you know what you get when you cross an elephant with a hooker?"

Mrs. Cavanaugh just continued to check carefully the suit's fit.

"You get a two-ton pickup," Fatso said with a giggle.

The two of them looked up when they heard the door bell jingle, indicating someone had just entered the store.

Fatso, looking a little embarrassed from wearing the Santa suit, said, "Well, well, if it isn't the Wong man!"

Mr. Wong Chang eyed the strange sight of Fatso and Mrs. Cavanaugh behind the checkout counter and said, "I need to speak with Mr. Green."

Fatso replied, "Okay Mr. Chang, but first you have to tell me what you call an elephant that flies?"

The expression on Mr. Chang's face did not change.

"An elephant that flies would be a jumbo jet," replied Fatso as he pressed the button to release the lock on Trigger Green's office. He then pointed toward the door and said, "Okay, go on back."

As Mr. Chang started walking toward Trigger's office Mrs. Cavanaugh said, "Okay Fatso, I'm satisfied with the fit. You can take it off now, but fold it carefully and make sure it stays looking good for the party on Saturday. I wouldn't want anyone to think I did shoddy work." She then turned, grabbed her purse, and headed toward the door.

"Thank you Mrs. Cavanaugh," Fatso said to her. "Where you headed in such a hurry?"

Mrs. Cavanaugh replied, "Got some shopping to do."

"You going to Wal-Mart?" asked Fatso.

Mrs. Cavanaugh said, "No, I'm going to Big Lots. You don't have to get dressed up to go there like you do for Wal-Mart." She went out the front door.

As Mr. Chang entered the office he was again greeted by an outstretched hand and Trigger Green's smiling face, "Welcome, welcome my friend. Really good to see you again.

Please have a seat and let's talk." Trigger then walked around and sat at his desk.

"I hope the citizens of our fair county are treating you well," Trigger said.

"Yes," replied Mr. Chang, "everyone has been very nice."

"So how's the plan going to kidnap Choe from the Slusher brothers?" Trigger asked.

"That's what I'm here for," replied Mr. Chang. "I need you to provide a little help."

Trigger said, "Hold up, now. Remember, I told you I would not take part in the kidnapping, and I meant it."

Mr. Chang replied, "No, no. I'm not asking for that kind of assistance. All I need from you is for Mr. Fatso to place a gift in his bag that will be addressed to Choe. I've decided that the best way to accomplish my mission is to give Choe a nice gift along with a card that asks him to please give me a call. When he calls me I will try and convince him to come meet me at my motel room. I'll tell him on the phone that I have urgent business with him from his family. I feel certain that he will agree to meet with me. Once he shows up at the motel I'll be able to either convince him to go back to North Korea with me willingly, or, if not, then I have a backup plan."

"So let me get this straight," Trigger said. "All you need from me is to ask Fatso to put a gift to Choe in his Santa bag for the party Saturday night?"

Mr. Chang said, "That is correct. That's all I need. And if you agree, I'll bring the gift to you on Saturday afternoon."

Trigger thought a moment and then said, "Well, the way

I figure it, once Choe opens that gift, calls you, and then goes to the Mountain Lair the two of you will be headed back to North Korea. So I'll agree to let Fatso take the gift only if you give me the balance of $10,000 on Saturday when you bring me Choe's gift."

"That was my intention," replied Mr. Chang.

Trigger smiled, rubbed his hands together, and said, "Mr. Chang, it's a great pleasure doing business with you. I'll look forward to seeing you Saturday, and we'll conclude our deal."

Mr. Chang smiled. The two men stood, shook hands, and Mr. Chang turned and left Trigger's office.

As he walked toward the front door Mr. Chang heard Fatso shout to him, "Hey Wong man, you know how to raise a baby elephant?"

Mr. Chang just kept walking toward the door.

"You raise a baby elephant with a fork-lift!" Fatso shouted with a laugh.

Mr. Chang left the store, got in his rental car, and started the drive back to his motel. As he drove he thought, *I've got two more days to get the bomb all assembled. I think I've already got all the materials I need. Then I just need to put it together in a box, wrap the box as a Christmas gift, and take it along with $10,000 to Trigger Green on Saturday. By the time Choe Yong-ho opens that gift I should be at the airport in Knoxville, Tennessee waiting on my flight home, and the six deserters will be history.*

Gunsmoke and Booger sat with Ray at their kitchen table. Gunsmoke said, "I'm sure not experienced on this party thing. So let's go over everything one more time. We're going to have a total of 21 people attending." Gunsmoke looked at his list and read, "The three of us, Charlie, George, the six Koreans, the sheriff, Fatso, Raymond and Betty Bell, Kyle and Carolyn Potter, Mayor Knapp, Rosie Cain, Dr. Randy Peters, and Gus Richenberger. Is that correct?"

Ray grinned and said, "You left one out!"

The brothers looked at Ray. Booger said, "Who might that be?"

Ray answered, "Rosie Cain's going to be bringing Preacher Puss."

"She ain't a person," Gunsmoke said. "But I know she thinks she is."

Booger grinned and said, "And she's most welcome. It'll really be good to see her. That alone will be a Christmas gift for me." Gunsmoke and Ray both nodded approvingly.

Gunsmoke said, "We'll make sure ole Preacher Puss gets several Whisker Lickin treats for Christmas!" Booger and Ray laughed.

"Better hope nobody pulls a gun out if Preacher Puss is around. That would sure spoil someone's holiday spirit," Booger said.

"Don't think that'll happen," replied Gunsmoke. "Okay,

back to business. So we got 21 people all together. Ray, you got gifts for everyone other than me and Booger, right?"

Ray replied, "Yep, I've got 19 gifts all wrapped real pretty and awaiting ole Fatso Santa's gift bag. In addition to those, there's a whole bunch more that myself, Charlie, George, and the Koreans wanted to give. So ole Santa's bag's going to be plenty full!"

"That sounds great," Gunsmoke replied. "So the plan is that Fatso should get here around 6 pm. He'll get his gift bag all packed and put on his Santa outfit. I thought it'd be good to have him wearing it during dinner. It will add to the Christmas spirit. So we'll have dinner at 7 pm. All the plans are set with the caterer for the food?"

"Yep," Ray replied. "They were told to be here at 6:30 and set up. Should be a great meal."

"So after the meal everyone will be asked to gather in the great room and Fatso Santa will distribute the gifts, is that correct?" asked Gunsmoke.

Ray said, "That's the plan. I think everything should be concluded by no later than 10 pm. So everyone should have no problem getting back home and all tucked in their beds to await the arrival of Christmas."

"One question," asked Booger. "What about the guard gate. We want Charlie and George both here for the party."

Ray replied, "Well, George will stay on the gate until all the guests have checked in. When the last one arrives, he'll lock-up the guard house and come on here to the party. No one else will be able to get in.....but in an emergency they could call us on the intercom. Course the gate opens automatically as folks leave, so that won't be a problem."

"Sounds to me like everything's covered," Gunsmoke said. "I just hope everything goes well and all have a great time. It's Christmas, and all need to be in the spirit of the season."

"Amen to that," Booger said. "Ray, you know what the weather forecast is for Christmas eve?"

"The good Lord is cooperating with us," replied Ray. "Forecast is for the low thirties with a chance of snow flurries. That's about perfect!"

The three men stood and shook hands. The party was all set.

Chapter 10

Washington, D.C.
The White House
December 22

President Cannon and his Director of National Intelligence, Susan Bean, were seated in the oval office. Director Bean sat on a couch, the President was behind his desk. He said, "Susan, our time is running down. What's the latest on the North Korean nuclear threat?"

She replied, "Everything seems to be running smoothly and right on time. Just yesterday we got an update from the Japanese government that gave a revised date of December 28th for the departure of the **_Taka Maru_**. It should arrive in Chongjin sometime on December 30th. It will then take on the North Korean crew and five containers that house the nuclear weapon and associated equipment. We have not been able to find out exactly when they plan to leave, but since they intend to deliver the weapon on Kim's birthday, January 8th, we assume they will leave no more than a couple of days after arriving."

President Cannon replied, "So if I understand everything correctly, General O must get to Ishigaki before December 28th. Is that correct?"

Director Bean said, "Yes. But we would like him there at least a couple of days ahead of the estimated departure date in case there were last minute changes, and also to give him a little time to rest before he starts the mission. So right now we have him scheduled out of Kentucky on Monday, December 26th."

"So is everything going okay with General O," the president asked?

"All is real good," replied Director Bean. "Our intelligence agents have been spending every afternoon with him since their arrival on December 2. They tell us that General O is very cooperative, and has been excellent to study all the information we've given him. He's completely up to date on every aspect of the mission."

The president said, "Well, that's fine and good, but we've got to have back-up plans in place in the event something goes wrong with General O."

"And we do, as you are aware," replied Susan Bean. "We will have one of our subs in the area, remaining far enough away from the *Taka Maru* that it will not be detected. If we receive word from General O that his mission has failed, the sub will torpedo the boat. Of course we would only do that as a last resort, since it would kill a lot of innocent people."

"But would save the lives of millions of Americans," said the president. "But what if General O is discovered and he can't let us know?"

"In that event we would just have to rely on our monitoring of the microphone that he wears," Director Bean replied. "We'll be listening to every word that is spoken anywhere around the General. If we detect he's been compromised, then we'll be forced to destroy the ship."

"Well, that gives us a couple of alternatives, but only as a last resort. I would certainly hope we could avoid having to take out the boat and all aboard," replied the president.

Susan Bean said, "Yes, I understand completely. Also, we have two other contingencies that you need to be aware of. While the **Taka Maru** has been in port at Ishigaki we convinced the Japanese government to allow us to place a container aboard the boat that contains enough explosives to destroy it. We simply told the Japanese that there was equipment in the container that was essential to the national security mission of Mr. Cho. They agreed to allow it. Our container was loaded along with several others that were being shipped to Venezuela. We have the explosives hooked up a state-of-the-art electronic system that can be activated by General O, aka Mr. Cho, by the captain of the sub that will be close by, or by myself or you, Mr. President. The advantage this has over the torpedo is that it could be activated faster. The last contingency is a team of four navy seals that will be aboard the sub. Should there arise a reason to use them they could launch an inflatable from the sub and could arrive at the ship in about 15 minutes. We don't anticipate needing them, but they'll be there just in case."

"Okay, so I think I understand the contingencies. But go over again exactly how General O will accomplish his mission if all goes as planned." requested President Cannon.

"Sure," replied Director Bean. "As we discussed, he will board the ship at Ishigaki probably on the 27th. Captain Saito has been instructed to receive him as an engineering officer and get him all settled aboard. Our intelligence agents have thoroughly briefed General O to allow him to pass with this identity. He, along with the entire crew of the **Taka Maru**, will be introduced to the 12 North Koreans that board at Chongjin. He has been instructed to be seen as little as possible without arousing suspicion. At some point after getting into the Pacific the North Koreans will take control of the ship and direct Captain Saito to sail a course toward the western coast of the U.S. Since all the ship officers are necessary to operate the vessel it is anticipated that General O will be allowed to function as usual. Resistance is not anticipated by the captain or crew. Prior to the ship arriving at its launch position General O will determine where the missile is being set-up along with its control console. When the ship stops in order to launch, General O will take whatever action is required to prevent the launch. We think no more than three North Koreans will be at the missile site, with the other nine distributed over the ship to make sure all is under control. The general is well capable of dealing with the three or so North Koreans. Once the missile is disabled the navy seals will be dispatched from the sub to come aboard and subdue the remaining North Koreans and return control of the ship to Captain Saito and crew."

"Sounds to me like we're really putting a lot of stock in General O. You really think he's up to this?" asked the president.

"I do," responded Susan Bean. "But if anything does go wrong, we have the contingencies. And as badly as we would hate to wipe out the entire ship and all aboard, it would easily be justified by saving the lives of millions of Americans. One way or another that nuclear warhead will not be allowed to launch for Los Angeles."

The president started to slowly nod his head affirmatively. He said, "I sure hope we've got all the bases covered.....the stakes are just too high for failure."

Pyongyang, North Korea

The intercom buzzed in Supreme Leader Kim Jong-un's office. "Yes?" said Kim

"Supreme Leader, you have a call from Admiral Sung Ho-Jun," replied Kim's secretary.

Kim laid down the Jelly doughnut he was just starting to eat, picked up his phone, and said, "Yes Admiral Sung. How's everything in Chongjin?"

Admiral Sung replied, "Good, Supreme Leader, very good. I'm sorry to bother you, but I had one question. As we discussed previously, I know you wish the launch to occur on your birthday, January 8th. But we had not discussed the exact time you had in mind."

Kim said, "Yes Admiral Sung. That is a good question. I will be so excited awaiting the birthday gift, I think I would like it presented at the exact time my birthday begins."

The Admiral replied, "Yes, I understand. So at exactly midnight in Pyongyang, between January 7th and 8th, we will launch the missile." Admiral Sung then looked at a time chart on the wall before him, and continued, "So that would correspond to 7:30 am in Los Angeles on January 7th. Once launched the missile will only take about 90 minutes to reach its target. Is that agreeable with you, Supreme Leader?"

Kim smiled and said, "Precisely what I want. It will be a birthday gift to be long remembered." Kim slammed down the phone, picked up the jelly doughnut, and stuffed it in his mouth.

Harlan County, Kentucky

Agents Clair Eaton and Rose McKay sat on one side of the kitchen table. General O sat on the opposite side. A huge pile of reports and papers rested on the table between them. They were in the kitchen of the Slusher brother's three bedroom guest house where Charlie, George, and Ray lived. The three had offered their residence for General O's daily meetings with the intelligence agents since the three employees would be working and the meetings could be held in confidence and without interruption.

Clair Eaton said, "General O, or perhaps we should start calling you Mr. Cho, Rose and I certainly appreciate your assistance and patience. I know we've gone over these details many times, but I hope you agree that it's been time well spent and we hope you are beginning to feel comfortable with your upcoming mission."

General O, aka Mr. Cho, replied, "You ladies have been wonderful. Although I knew much about North Korea's military and nuclear program, the information you have provided has been extremely valuable. I feel very comfortable with my new identity as Mr. Cho, and I feel I'll be able to carry out the mission. All my identification and papers seem to be in order. You have done a good job."

"Thank you Mr. Cho," said Rose McKay. "We've had a tremendous amount of help and support from Washington. We'll only meet with you one more day, and then we want you to enjoy Christmas eve and Christmas day. You will then leave on Monday morning, December 26th on your mission. Clair and I will drive you to the Knoxville airport. Although we won't formally meet on Saturday and Sunday, the two of us will be working at our motel should you need us."

"You don't get off for Saturday and Sunday?" asked General O.

"Nope," replied Clair Eaton. "National security doesn't take a holiday. But after we drive you to Knoxville on Monday we'll be taking a few days off. It's not a problem for us."

Chapter 11

Lexington, Kentucky
December 22

Yes, Joyce," Dr. Randy Peters said into his intercom as he sat at his desk at the University of Kentucky's Center for Appalachian Research (CAR), where he served as its director.

"You have a phone call from an Agent Clair Eaton. She says she needs to talk with you immediately on a matter of great urgency," replied Joyce, Dr. Peter's secretary.

"Yes, please put her call through to me," responded Randy Peters.

"Good afternoon, Agent Eaton, how may I help you?" Dr. Peters asked

Clair Eaton said, "Good afternoon to you, Dr. Peters. You know my name, but let me add that I'm an agent with national intelligence. I and another agent are in Harlan County on a matter of great national importance. I know that you are very familiar with the situation involving the six North Koreans that are now staying at the Slusher brothers' farm."

"Yes, I certainly am," replied Randy. "I hope there's not a problem with them or their political asylum status."

Agent Eaton replied, "No, not at all. As a matter of fact, General O has been tagged to voluntarily assist us in our urgent mission. And just this afternoon he disclosed to us a request that must have your approval."

"I see," replied Dr. Peters. "If that's the case, then I think I can guess that the request must somehow involve one or more of the anchor crosses that I have in my possession."

"You are most perceptive," Clair Eaton responded. "I know that you are aware that all six of the North Koreans were well briefed about the anchor crosses before they were sent here by Kim Jong-un in an attempt to steal them. So they are most knowledgeable about them and their apparent mysterious power. General O has requested that he be allowed to temporarily wear one of the anchor crosses while on a mission he will begin next Monday. He said that Harlan County Sheriff's Deputy Kyle Potter owns one of the six anchor crosses you currently have in your center for study and research, and that perhaps Deputy Potter would permit him to borrow his Seibert anchor cross."

"Have you asked Kyle Potter?" inquired Randy.

"Not yet," Clair Eaton said. "I wanted to first check with you. I feel pretty confident that Deputy Potter will agree. But it's of utmost importance that we be able to physically have the Seibert anchor cross here for General O prior to his departure on Monday. With Kyle's approval, can you help us with this?"

Randy replied, "Absolutely. As a matter of fact, I have an invitation to the Christmas eve party at the Slusher brothers' farm. I was planning on driving to Harlan on Saturday for the party, and was invited to stay overnight with my good friends Pastor Raymond and Betty Bell. With Kyle's consent I could bring the artifact with me and give it to General O at the party. I know he'll be attending also."

Clair Eaton said, "That will be wonderful. What you just suggested was exactly what I had planned to ask of you. We knew, of course, about the party and that you were invited. After we finish our conversation I'll contact Deputy Potter and explain the situation to him and ask for his approval. I'll request that he phone you to confirm his okay."

"I'll look forward to receiving his call," said Randy. "It's been a pleasure chatting with you and I'm glad I could be of service. I hope General O's mission is successful. All six of those North Koreans are very special people."

"I agree," Agent Eaton said. "I thank you so much for your help. Good-bye."

Randy hung up his phone and thought, *Since the arrival of those anchor crosses things certainly have gotten interesting around here.*

———————

Harlan County, Kentucky

General O sat in the Lounge chair in his bedroom. He was deep in thought about his upcoming trip. He had gotten a phone call just a few minutes earlier from Clair Eaton telling him that everything looked good for his getting the Seibert anchor cross to wear on his mission. That made him feel much better. From all he knew about the artifact it would certainly aid him from being harmed. He realized that chances were good that he would need that protection. He also knew that the odds on stopping the missile and getting back home safely were not good. He knew about the contingencies, and he knew if he could not disable the missile he and all aboard the ship would be destroyed. That risk he just had to take. He wanted to do all within his power to save the millions of people in Los Angeles and to prevent the madman Kim Jong-un from getting his birthday wish. It would be a wonderful gift he could give to his new country. His head slowly dropped as he dozed off for a nap.

Harlan, Kentucky

Bert, Kyle, and Fred all sat together drinking coffee at Creech Cafe. It was late in the day, but the friends frequently got together at day's end to review what had happened.

Mayor Knapp said, "So one of those North Koreans will

be borrowing your anchor cross, huh Kyle?" Deputy Potter had just explained to Bert and Fred his phone call from Agent Eaton.

Kyle replied, "I really had no choice, Fred. When you get a request from a national intelligence agent how could you say no?"

Bert laughed and said, "You could have denied it Kyle.....and then Fred and I would have come to visit you in Leavenworth".

"That's not funny, Bert," Kyle replied. "I have no problem at all loaning my anchor cross for an important national mission. I do wish I knew what the mission was, just out of curiosity."

The sheriff replied, "Well, that's not going to happen. Anything as high up as whatever this mission is will be made known only to those with a need-to-know, and that doesn't include us."

Bert and Kyle nodded in agreement.

A loud burst of laughter came from the other end of the cafe. The three men turned to see what was so funny, and saw Minnie Johnson bent over in laughter. Fred said, "I better go check on Minnie." He stood and walked toward her.

As Fred walked beside Minnie he saw she had read an article that he had recently posted on his wall. It was from the **Harlan Daily Enterprise** and had a picture of a little girl looking up inquisitively at her mother. The caption under the photograph said, 'Mommy, where did I come from?' The article read:

At last Saturday's meeting of the Harlan Bridge

Club Wanda Noe shared the following story. My nine-year old daughter Sally was recently involved in some discussions at school related to where she came from. When she got home she asked me, "Mother, where did I come from?" I answered, "Honey, it says in the Bible that in the beginning God created the heavens and the earth. It goes on to say that He created Adam and Eve, the first man and women, and then they had children, their children had children, and so forth. That's where you came from." Sally thanked me and then when her father got home she asked him the same question. He answered her by saying, "Honey, over in Africa a long time ago there was this bunch of apes and monkeys. They kept breeding and eventually we evolved from them. That's where you came from." Sally thanked her father, and came back and told me what her father had just told her. Sally then asked me, "So Mommy, I don't know where I came from." I said, "Well, honey, it's like this. Your father was talking about his side of the family and I was talking about mine!"

Mrs. Johnson looked at Fred, slapped him on the back, and said, "Mayor, that's really a funny one."

"Glad you enjoyed it, Minnie," Fred replied. "Not only out of the mouths of babes oft times come gems, but also out of the mouths of babes' mothers."

"You're a jewel, Fred," Replied Minnie Johnson as she started walking toward the door.

Chapter 12

Washington, D.C.
December 22

Jon Kennan, Director of the CIA, was meeting with General Herman Jackson. The meeting was taking place in the pentagon. General Jackson was the military's leading expert on missile systems. The two had just taken seats in a secure conference room.

"General Jackson, I appreciate your taking the time to meet with me. I know you have briefed my people on your knowledge of North Korea's missiles, but I just had a few questions, if you don't mind."

"Certainly, Director Kennan," replied the general. "Glad to be of assistance."

Kennan said, "So, you're reasonably certain that the missile the North Koreans will use in the attempted nuclear strike will be a Russian Kalibr?"

"Yes," replied the general. "Our sources tell us that they have acquired several of the Russian 3M-54 Klub cruise-type surface-to-surface missiles. They can carry a nuclear warhead, and could likely achieve the mission as I understand it."

"I see," said Director Kennan. "What can you tell me about the range of this missile?"

General Jackson said, "Well, they have a range of up to about 1500 miles. There are many variations, so it would be very difficult to know exactly. Depends on the type of engine also."

"Would it be safe to say that about 1500 miles would be the maximum range?" asked Director Keenan.

"I think so," replied the general.

"What I'm trying to establish is how far out from our west coast the ship could fire the missile," Director Keenan replied. "If we know this, then we can better estimate when the strike will occur."

"I understand. I'd say you probably should assume they would want a good factor of safety. So I would recommend you think about 1000 miles. Further than this could possibly cause them problems. I think you should consider them likely to fire when they get about 1000 miles out."

"It's a little under 6,000 miles from Chongjin to Los Angeles. We think their ship will steam at about 25 knots." Director Keenan pulled out a calculator and punched in some numbers. "If I'm figuring right, that means that to cover 5,000 miles would take about 8 days. So that would mean that 8 days from when they weighed anchor they could be close enough to LA to launch the missile."

"That sounds about right," said General Jackson. "Do you know when they intend to leave Chongjin?"

"No, but we do know that Kim Jong-un's birthday is January 8th. So my guess would be that they would leave no later than January 1, since the punk dictator wants the nuclear strike as his birthday present."

The two looked grimly at each other.

***

Chongjin, North Korea

Admiral Sung and Commander Shin sat huddled about a table covered with nautical charts.

The Admiral said, "Shin, our Supreme Leader says he wants the missile delivered at the strike of midnight when his birthday arrives." He pointed to the red line drawn on the chart. "If we follow this course, and all goes well, we should arrive at this point at the launch time. It is well within the missile's range, and I think it would be safe to plan the launch from there. Do you agree?"

Lieutenant Commander Shin looked at the spot on the chart marked with a red X, thought carefully, and said, "Yes Admiral, I think that would work fine. We will need to take command of the ship after about one day at sea in order to stay on your desired course. And then if we do not encounter any mechanical problems or heavy weather we certainly should be able to make our target in time for launch."

Admiral Sung replied, "Good. Good. I'm pleased you agree. I'll phone the Supreme Leader tomorrow to confirm our plans."

Chapter 13

Harlan County, Kentucky
December 23

Badass Brown sat in his dilapidated trailer. He had just finished wrapping the 'gift' that Bennie would be presenting to Sheriff Sterling, and it now rested on the coffee table in front of him. He had used a shoe box, and had carefully cut out one end of the box. The squirt gun filled with sulfuric acid would be placed in that open end. The rest of the box he had carefully wrapped with bright red Christmas paper, and then had put a big green bow on the top of the box. Badass looked at it approvingly. He reached with his left hand, grabbed the side of the box, and raised it off the coffee table. He then used his right hand to grab the squirt gun that had been resting beside the gift box and placed the gun in the open end of the box that was toward him. Satisfied that the gun fit easily into the box, he then quickly removed the gun with his right hand and pointed it straight ahead after releasing the box with his left hand and said, "Christmas gift Bert". Badass then got a big grin on his face and thought, *the sheriff will either be dead or blinded. A great Christmas gift for me!*

The agents sat with General O at his kitchen table. Clair Eaton said, "Well, General O, today will be our last briefing session. When we leave today we'll next see you bright and early on Monday morning for our trip to the Knoxville airport. I think we've pretty much conveyed all the information that you'll need for your mission. The last thing we needed to do today was to give you some hardware and explain its use." Agent Eaton then reached inside her brief case and extracted a box which she placed on the table.

"I bet that's not a Christmas gift," General O said.

"Not exactly," Agent Rose McKay replied. "But we do think you'll find it interesting!"

Agent McKay then opened the box to reveal a beautiful men's watch. She said, "Okay, General O, this is your new watch. It's kind of special. As a matter of fact, it's real special."

General O removed the watch he was wearing, and slipped the new watch around his left wrist. He said, "Looks very nice. But you say it's real special?"

"Correct," said Clair Eaton. "It is VERY special. First off, the watch has a super sensitive microphone in it. We'll be monitoring everything that you say or hear. If you wish to send us a quick message, just talk into your watch. We'll hear it. Let me also say that the submarine will also be monitoring. Should any of the bad guys cause a problem, we'll hear that as well. Secondly, if you remove the watch you'll notice on its back side an indented cap that looks like where you would replace a battery."

General O then removed the watch and looked at it's back side. He said, "Yes, I see it. The indented cap has a slot in it where a coin or screw driver would go to remove it."

"Exactly," Agent Eaton replied. "But that's not at all what it is. If that cap is pressed three times within two seconds a signal is sent to the explosives aboard the ship. That signal would cause the explosives to detonate resulting in the total destruction of the ship, cargo, and crew......including you."

General O replied, "Well, I guess I wouldn't want to do that except as a very last resort."

"Precisely correct," said Agent Eaton. "And that's why it has to be pressed three times in succession, to make sure that it's not accidently used. You would only use it if all your other efforts failed and you wanted to save the lives of millions of people as well as the start of World War III. Certainly we don't expect that will be necessary, but we did want you to know that it's an option."

"I understand," General O replied. "I feel confident I'll be able to disable the missile without the need to destroy the boat and crew, but I do understand the necessity for the backup.". He then placed the watch back on his wrist. "Anything else with this watch?"

Agent McKay said, "One other thing. Should you need to talk with us we're giving you a satellite phone." She then reached in the brief case, pulled out the phone, and handed it to General O. "For security reasons, the phone can be used for outgoing calls only after we have approved such. We've done this to make sure that if the phone is discovered by the bad guys they can't identify us. You can call us by two different ways. One way is to simply talk into your watch and say you need to call us. We'll then activate the satellite phone for your call. If we don't get the call within one minute we'll deactivate it again. The other way you can use the phone is to press the number 7 on the keypad three times within 2 seconds. Sort of like pressing the cap on the watch. When this happens, we will receive your call within the next one minute. After that, the phone becomes deactivated again. We have this second option just in case something happens to your watch."

General O replied, "Got it. That makes me feel better. If I really had need to talk with you I could."

"Yes," said Agent McKay. "But only if absolutely needed. We have to assume that the bad guys might be monitoring on the ship as well. And if you're seen and/or heard talking into your watch or on your phone your cover could be blown."

"Understood," said General O. "And I assume you have some voice recognition software in place that would eliminate someone else from trying to use my watch or phone."

Clair Eaton said, "Yes, General O, that is correct. Only your voice will be recognized."

"Any other hardware?" the general asked.

"That's it," answered Agent Eaton. "The only other piece of hardware will not be arriving until the Christmas Eve party tomorrow evening. Dr. Randy Peters will be bringing the Seibert anchor cross that you requested. From everything we've read we understand it to be stunningly beautiful. We highly recommend you wear it under your shirt so that it cannot be seen. Otherwise you might get conked on the head and have the beautiful golden artifact stolen."

"Yes, I had already planned to wear it under my clothes," said General O.

Rose McKay then said, "That's about everything. Clair and I will be leaving now, and we'll be here to pick you up on Monday morning around 6 am. We hope you have a great Christmas party tomorrow night, and a wonderful Christmas day on Sunday."

Both agents extended their hands to General O. He gave them both a hug instead, and said, "I'm sorry you won't be coming to the party, but I understand that duty comes first. So I'll just wish you a big Merry Christmas and look forward to starting the mission with you bright and early on Monday morning."

General O watched as the agents left for their car.

Trigger Green stood behind the Maggard's grocery check-out counter talking with Fatso Chapel, "Fatso, tomorrow's the big party at the Slusher brothers' farm. I needed to talk with you about that.

"Sure, boss," Fatso replied. "But before we get to that, tell me why elephants paint their testicles red."

Trigger stared at Fatso.

Fatso said, "So they can hide in cherry trees."

Trigger continued to stare at Fatso.

"Okay, okay," Fatso said. "We can get down to business now."

Trigger said, "We have a client, Mr. Wong Chang, who wants you to deliver a Christmas gift to one of the North Koreans. He'll stop tomorrow to leave it. The gift goes to Choe Yong-ho. You are to place the gift in your Santa gift bag and distribute it along with all the other gifts. Mr. Chang has been retained by Choe's family to try and talk him into coming back home to North Korea. The gift has a note in it for him to phone Mr. Chang. That's the way Mr. Chang wants to do it, and he's paying us handsomely. Mr. Chang says it has to be a total surprise. No one is to know about it, and neither you or I are to reveal any of this to anyone. It's lips sealed. You understand?"

"I'm not stupid, Trigger. Of course I understand," replied Fatso.

"So what time are you going to the party tomorrow?" asked Trigger.

Fatso said, "They told me to be there at 6. So I figured I'd leave here soon after I close the store at 5. Might get there a little early, but that'd be okay."

"Well, you look for Mr. Chang tomorrow. He'll be bringing the gift by. You just go ahead and put it in your Santa gift bag when you get it so you won't forget. Okay?"

"Sounds like a plan to me," Fatso responded. Trigger turned to walk away as Fatso continued, "Hey Trigger, You know what weighs four tons and is bright red?"

Trigger continued walking.

"An elephant holding his breath," Fatso said with a chuckle.

———

General Park Chang-sun, aka Mr. Wong Chang, sat on the bed in his Mount Lair motel room carefully examining the bomb he had assembled to look like a Christmas gift. All the explosives he needed he had gotten from Pretty Boy Maggard when the two met in Knoxville upon his arrival. Everything else he had been able to purchase locally without any problem. The main concern was to make the gift as light as possible, so it would not be suspect. If he had used steel pipes and steel ball bearings it would have been very heavy. Instead, he was able to find aluminum pipe and ball bearings. Much lighter, but would do the job just fine. When the explosives were set off the metal from the pipes would be shredded and it, along with the ball bearings, would go flying in every direction.....lethal to anyone in their path. He looked at his handiwork. Inside the gift box he was able to get four pipes, each about one foot long with end caps and filled with a mixture of the deadly explosive and ball bearings. He had a detonator wired through the cap on one of the pipe bombs. When activated it would set off a spark in the bomb that would trigger explosions of all four. The tricky part was to wire the lid of the box such that when Choe removed it a wire would be pulled and touch a battery that would activate the detonator. Before he left for the U.S. General Park had received instruction in North Korea about how to put the bomb together. He had practiced by making three such bombs, and they all worked exactly as planned. He felt very confident.

General Park carefully assembled the lid on the box, making certain that the critical activator wire was positioned correctly. Satisfied with it, he then carefully wrapped the Christmas gift in a metallic green wrapping paper with red ribbon and bow. He taped a card to the top of the box that read, 'To Choe Yong-ho'. He then placed the attractive gift in a plastic grocery bag to carry to Maggard's grocery tomorrow.

Tonight he would call Kim Jong-un and report his progress. He would tell Kim that if all went as planned he should be back in Pyongyang no later than December 26. His plan was to leave for Knoxville as soon as he dropped the gift-bomb off at Maggard's grocery tomorrow. He had reservations leaving on a flight from Knoxville on Sunday morning, Christmas day. He would spend Saturday night with Pretty Boy Maggard. They would watch the evening news to confirm the bombing in Harlan county. If all went well he would be on his way Sunday morning to North Korea and his reward. If the bomb failed, he would be on his way back to Harlan County to come up with another plan. He could not go home without success. To do so was certain death.

Chapter 14

Harlan, Kentucky
December 24

Bennie had just gotten in Badass Brown's old converted bread truck. Badass started driving and said, "Bennie, you don't look too good. You okay?"

"I don't normally get up this early....usually sleep till about noon," Bennie replied.

Badass said, "Well, you got a job to do this morning, and I don't want any screw-up's. Do you feel up to it?"

"If you got the fifty bucks and the gallon of 'shine, I'm ready," Bennie said.

"I got that," replied Badass. "But you gotta earn it. You must do everything just the way I'm going to show you. You think you can do that?"

"Of course I can," Bennie said.

The two then sat quietly as Badass continued the drive to the court house.

Bennie said, "Sure won't have any trouble parking this morning. The streets look deserted."

"Christmas eve," Badass replied. "Not too many folks working today, but lucky for us the sheriff's office will be open till noon."

Badass found a parking spot for his old bread truck on Central Street, just east of the court house. He parked so he could see the entrance door to the sheriff's office, located on the east side of the court house building. The two then got out of the truck and walked around to the back door, opened it, stepped up inside, and shut the door. The old converted bread truck had windows that allowed light inside.

Badass reached over to a shelf and removed the Christmas gift wrapped in bright red paper with a big green bow.

"Wow," Bennie exclaimed, "that's pretty. But it's got a hole in one end!"

"Shut up, Bennie, and listen and watch," demanded Badass. "We're going to practice this several times until I feel like you got it down." He then reached over to another shelf and grabbed the water pistol filled with sulfuric acid and placed it in the box through the open end. Then with both hands holding the gift box he stretched it straight in front of him and said, "Now you'll walk into the sheriff's office holding the gift like this. You must remember to keep it level or the gun will slip out. Deputy Rosie Cain will be there and ask what you want. You tell her you have this gift that you would like to deliver to Sheriff Sterling. She'll likely then ask you to wait until she gets him. He'll then come into the front office and walk over to you. When he's standing right in front of you, you continue to hold the gift with your left hand and with your right hand reach in and grab the gun, like this," Badass demonstrated the move and then continued, "You pull the gun out and let the box drop to the floor and then squirt Bert right directly in the face as you shout 'Christmas gift!', you got that?"

"Yeah," Bennie replied. "And then I just turn and run out the door and come back to your truck to get my fifty bucks and the gallon of moonshine, right?"

"Correct," said Badass. "Now let's practice a few times to make sure you got it down."

Bennie then was handed the box and gun, and they practiced the entire gift-giving act for four times. Then Badass said, "Okay, I think you've got it. It's show-time Bennie....now don't mess this up. Just think about the fifty bucks and shine you'll earn if you do it right."

Badass then looked through the truck windows to see if anyone was outside. Seeing no one, he opened the back door and the two of them stepped out. He then walked around and got in the truck's driver's seat, and watched as Bennie walked toward the court house with the gift carefully being carried level in front of him. Badass thought, *Now I'll just sit here and wait and watch. If it goes well, then ole Bennie will come running out, get in my truck, and we'll be off. If it doesn't go well, then I'll just drive off and Bennie will have to concoct some kind of story. That'll be his problem. Surely it'll work this time. Merry Christmas Bert!*

Deputy Rosie Cain was standing behind the counter working on the sheriff's department payroll sheets. She had just finished filling Preacher Puss's water and food trays and had walked over to where the cat was napping on her cushioned-ledge above the desk beside the entrance door. Preacher Puss perked up her ears and looked at Rosie expectantly. Rosie gave her several long strokes, and the cat responded by purring and swishing her tail gently. As soon as Rosie walked back behind the counter Preacher Puss immediately closed her eyes, curled her tail about her, and continued to nap. Rosie then heard the entrance door open. She looked up and saw the strange sight of ole Bennie standing there holding up in front of him a red and green Christmas gift.

Rosie said, "Well, Merry Christmas to you Bennie. Looks like you got a gift there."

Bennie replied, "Morning Rosie. Yeah, I got a special gift for Sheriff Sterling. I'd like to personally give it to him. Could you get him?"

Rosie laughed and said, "No problem, Bennie. You just wait there and I'll see if Bert's available." She turned and walked into the sheriff's office behind her.

Bennie went over in his mind exactly what he was to do. He then thought about the reward that awaited him, and that put a smile on his face. He just had to get this right. It wasn't hard....he knew he could do it!

"Well, well, if it isn't Bennie Sekao. Merry Christmas, Bennie," the sheriff said as he exited his office and walked around to where Bennie was standing beside the entrance door. "What do you have there?"

Bennie's voice was a little shaky as he said, "Morning Bert, just got a little Christmas gift for you." He then moved his right hand inside the box through the opening in the back of the gift, with his left hand still holding the box level. Next he grabbed the gun in his right hand, pulled it out, and let the box drop to the floor. He pointed the gun directly toward Bert's face.

Preacher Puss had been awakened from her nap, had sat up on her ledge, and had been carefully watching the man below her that was holding a bright red and green package. She thought it might possibly contain some kind of gift for her. Then she saw him pull out the gun.

Bennie's trigger finger was just getting ready to flex and squirt the sheriff, and he was just starting to say 'Christmas gift' when his world went black and the most excruciating pain was felt from his head. Blood started running down his face, across which Preacher Puss' tail swishing back and forth spread the blood evenly. Her claws were deeply wedged into his head atop which she sat facing backwards. Bennie screamed, "Help me! Help me!", and immediately released the squirt gun, allowing it to fall to the floor. When that happened, Preacher Puss retracted her claws and jumped from Bennie's head back to her shelf, curled up, closed her eyes, and continued her nap.

Bennie fell to his knees and reached up to hold his head. Blood squirted between his fingers. Sheriff Sterling and Rosie Cain both ran to Bennie to try and help.

Bert said, "Bennie, are you okay? Rosie, grab the first-aid kit." Bert helped Bennie up to sit in the chair of the deputy's desk. The sheriff pulled out his handkerchief and wiped some of the blood from Bennie's face and then pressed the handkerchief over the wounds on his head.

Rosie arrived with the first aid kit and the two of them put antiseptic on the wounds and then taped gauze over them. Bennie just sat with a glazed look on his face.

"How you doing," said the sheriff.

Bennie slowly replied, "I don't feel so hot. I was just trying to play a little trick on you Bert. Just going to squirt you with my squirt gun and say 'Christmas gift' when that damn creature attacked me again."

Rosie couldn't help grinning. She reached up and gave Preacher Puss a nice pet.

Bert said, "Bennie, this makes three times you've come into this office and pulled out some kind of gun. You should have known better. You know Preacher Puss doesn't tolerate guns. Why did you do it?"

Bennie just slowly shook his head, and mumbled, "I wasn't thinking, I guess."

On two previous occasions a few years back Bennie had pulled a gun while positioned below Preacher Puss with like results. His inebriated brain just didn't recall her presence.

Bennie saw the squirt gun on the floor beside him and reached down, grabbed it, and quickly put it in his pocket before Preacher Puss could repeat an attack. He said, "Sorry sheriff. I didn't mean nothing. Just a little Christmas gag. Can I go now?"

Bert looked at Bennie and said, "Bennie, it's Christmas eve. So you're free to go. But I'd advise you to head straight home, get cleaned up, and just get some rest."

Rosie said, "Merry Christmas, Bennie. I hope ole Santa comes to see you."

Bennie stood, turned, looked up at Preacher Puss like he wanted to wring her neck, and said, "Thanks. You all have a good Christmas." He then walked out the door.

Bert looked at Rosie and said with a smile, "Rosie, chalk up another one for Preacher Puss! You'd think that after two encounters ole Bennie would know that drawn guns bring on Preacher Puss' wrath. I guess it's the booze that causes him to forget."

Rosie laughed and said, "I guess. But you'd think after going through all that pain he'd remember. Hard to figure." Rosie bent over and picked up the gift box that had fallen to the floor and said, "You know, Bert, this box is wrapped awfully nice. I don't think Bennie could do that."

"Yeah, you're probably right. He likely had some help.... maybe from his friend Badass Brown. But it's hard to understand why they'd go to all that trouble just to squirt me. But then those two are hard to figure out."

Badass couldn't believe his eyes. What he saw walking toward his truck looked like Bennie, but there was blood all over his face and bandages covering his head. He looked like he had been through war. His first thought was to start up the truck and get out of Dodge. But then he noticed that no one was following him, and he wasn't even running....just slowly walking toward me. Curiosity made Badass wait to hear the story.

As he approached the truck Badass yelled through the window, "Hurry up, get in here. Let's get going."

Bennie opened the passenger-side door and got in the truck. Badass started the engine and started driving. He said, "Okay, what happened?"

Bennie told the story as best he could.

"Are you telling me you stood there and let that pussy cat attack you for the third time?"

"I forgot she was there," replied Bennie. "Can't remember everything!"

"You can't remember anything," said Badass.

"Do I still get my reward, Badass?" asked Bennie.

"Reward hell, I should shoot you rather than reward you," replied Badass. Just then Badass smelled something funny and looked toward Bennie. He saw a stream of smoke coming up from the seat area on Bennie's right side. "What's that smoke?"

Bennie looked down at his right front pocket and saw smoke coming through a hole in his pants pocket. He reached into his pocket and pulled out the gun. Drops of liquid were falling from it, and when they hit the seat they formed a hole and swirls of smoke wisped up. "What's that?" Bennie shouted.

Badass grabbed the gun, rolled down his driver side window, and threw it out. The gun rolled into the grass beside the road.

"Hey Badass, what was that all about?" Bennie asked.

"Nothing to worry about now," replied Badass as he continued to drive.

"Okay, Bennie, this is where you get out," Badass said as he pulled the truck to the curb.

"I still want my reward," Bennie replied.

Badass reached in his pocket and pulled out a twenty dollar bill, gave it to Bennie, and said, "If it wasn't Christmas I wouldn't do this. Now go."

Bennie took the twenty and got out of the truck. As Badass continued driving toward home he thought, *That damn sheriff's not going to get away that easy. I know he'll be leaving his office around noon. I think I'll come up with a little surprise for him, and this time it'll work. He won't live to see Christmas day.*

———

Harlan County, Kentucky

Fatso looked out the grocery store window and saw Wong Chang's car in the parking lot. He had been expecting him. Mr. Chang got out of the car and started walking toward the store with a grocery bag in his hand.

"Well, well, I do believe it's the Wong man," Fatso said as Mr. Chang entered the store.

"I need to again see Mr. Green," Mr. Chang said to Fatso.

"You're in luck. He's in," replied Fatso. "You know what's big and grey and red?"

Mr. Chang stood before Fatso at the check-out counter without emotion on his face.

"A sunburnt elephant," said Fatso with a chuckle as he pressed the button to open the lock on Trigger's office door. He then pointed toward the door and said, "Go right on back."

Mr. Chang, aka General Park, turned and walked toward Trigger's office.

"Ahh, Mr. Chang, so good to see you again," said Trigger Green as the two shook hands.

After taking their seats, Trigger behind his desk and Mr. Chang in front of the desk, Mr. Chang said, "Thank you Mr. Green," and he took the gift out of the plastic grocery bag and placed it on Trigger's desk. "Here's the gift that Mr. Fatso is to place in his Santa bag and deliver to Mr. Choe at the party tonight."

Trigger said, "That will be taken care of, Mr. Chang. And now, do you have a little Christmas gift for me?"

Mr. Chang reached into his coat pocket and pulled out an envelope. He handed it to Trigger and said, "You'll find $10,000 in there. Merry Christmas!"

Trigger took the envelope, opened it and flipped through the one hundred dollar bills, and said, "Mighty good gift it is, Mr. Chang. I thank you very much."

"It has been good doing business with you Mr. Green. I hope things work out for Mr. Choe and that he and I will be leaving very soon for North Korea." Mr. Chang then stood, turned, and walked out the door of Trigger's office.

"Hey Wong man, you know why the elephant stood on the marshmallow?" shouted Fatso as Mr. Chang walked rapidly toward the entrance door.

"Because he didn't want to fall into the hot chocolate!" shouted Fatso.

Mr. Chang slammed the door, walked to his car, got in and drove off.

Fatso, watching Mr. Chang leave the parking lot, thought to himself, *I wonder why he didn't turn in the direction of Harlan?*

General Park thought as he drove toward Knoxville, *I'm sure glad to be all finished dealing with that Mr. Fatso. He and his corny jokes will be history tonight along with all the deserters and their friends. My mission is just about finished. One more night in Knoxville with Pretty Boy Maggard and then home tomorrow. Mission accomplished.*

Harlan, Kentucky

It was almost noon. Badass Brown was parked in his converted bread van about a block away from the court house. It was time to execute his latest plan. He knew the sheriff's department was to shut down at noon. He knew the sheriff's car....it was parked in his reserved spot beside the court house. He knew it was always left unlocked. Badass had managed to get a pistol from a friend, and he had stuck it in his belt. At exactly 11:45 am he would walk to Bert's car and get in the back seat. At almost noon he would stretch out and lie face down on the back seat floorboard. That way the sheriff wouldn't notice him when he got in his cruiser. After he had driven a little ways out of town Badass would slowly rise up and stick the gun in the back of his head and tell him to drive up toward Martin's Fork lake. He'd make him pull over when they got to the lake, shoot him, and then dump his body into the water. Sweet revenge! He looked at his watch, it said 11:45. He better get started.

Sheriff Sterling came into the front office and said to Rosie, "Getting close to noon, and I think we've had enough action for the day. Just about got shot with a water pistol, and ole Preacher Puss once more saved the day! How about we shut down the office and try and enjoy the rest of Christmas eve."

Rosie looked a little concerned, and said, "I got a little problem, Bert."

The sheriff replied, "And what might that be?"

Rosie said, "I just got a phone call from my sister, Posey. She was helping me with my car. It had a problem and she had taken it to get it fixed for me. She dropped me off this morning and then was suppose to pick me up at noon, but she said the mechanic had to order a part for my car and it wouldn't be in until Monday. So I'm stuck!"

"Not to worry, Rosie, I've got a solution for you. Carolyn can pick me up here later this afternoon, I've got a little more work to do. You go ahead and take my car and use it over the weekend. I have my private car at home, so I'll have no problem. I'll see you and Preacher Puss at the party tonight."

"Oh Bert, you're an angel," Rosie said.

"Not really, but thanks for saying so," Bert said as he turned and went back into his office.

Rosie walked over to the keyboard and picked up the extra set of keys to Bert's cruiser. She then grabbed a bag of Whisker Lickins for Preacher Puss and put them in her purse. She then got the collar and leash for the cat, and put them on. Preacher Puss immediately knew that she was going to get to go out. She started purring loudly and swishing her tail about. Rosie said, "Now Preacher Puss, you just calm down. We're going home to get all cleaned up for the big party tonight. And you get to go. Everyone at the Slusher farm's looking forward to seeing you."

Rosie put on her coat, and then grabbed Preacher Puss in her arms. She knew the cat wouldn't walk with her on the leash. She just wanted it on her in case she needed to restrain her or park her somewhere. She picked up her purse and headed for the door.

Badass looked at his watch. Time to make myself invisible, he thought. He stretched out flat on the floorboard of the sheriff's cruiser and waited.

Shortly he heard someone outside the car, and then heard the front door open. The person got in and placed something in the passenger's seat. Badass figured that was likely his briefcase. The motor was started, the car backed out of its parking space onto the street, and then continued on its journey. Badass figured he'd wait until the car got out of the city limits before he made his move.

After about 5 minutes Badass very slowly pulled his gun from his belt. He then quietly began to raise up from the floorboard. He held the gun right in front of his face. When his head got just about to the top of the driver's seat he slowly raised the gun toward the back of the driver's head. It was at that exact moment that he saw the pointed ears and the piercing round eyes looking directly at him. Before he had time to react Preacher Puss pushed off from the armrest and flew through the air, clamping her claws around the hand holding the gun. Preacher Puss screamed, Badass screamed, and Rosie almost lost control of the car. Badass tried to get the cat off his hand and wrist by violently swinging the arm around. But Preacher Puss stayed put. The motion caused the claws to dig in deeper, and the pain was so intense that Badass lost consciousness. He dropped the gun and fell against the back seat with blood spurting from the wound. Rosie pulled the car to the shoulder of the road, slammed it into park, opened her door and jumped out. She opened the back door, grabbed her handcuffs, and placed them on Badass. She then grabbed the first aid kit from the car's trunk and put bandages over the wounds. She pulled Badass up in a sitting position and fastened the seat belt around him, and then got back under the wheel. She looked over at Preacher Puss. She was curled up in the passenger seat sound asleep! Rosie gave her a nice pet and said, "Preacher Puss, I don't know how we could get along without you. Let's get this bad guy to jail." She turned the car around and headed back toward the court house.

"Bert, are you still here," Rosie yelled as she pushed Badass Brown through the front door of the sheriff's department.

"Yeah, Rosie, still here. I thought you had left for the day." Bert shouted back from his office.

"You better come out here. I've got us a customer," she said.

Bert came walking through the door to his office and saw the two of them. "My, my, Rosie, it looks like you've apprehended Badass Brown. What was he up to?"

"He stuck a revolver in the back of my head. He was hiding in the back seat. Probably waiting on you. Preacher Puss was riding on the armrest and saw the pistol. You can likely guess what happened next," said an excited Rosie.

Bert took a look at the bandages around Badass's hand and said, "Yep, I can just picture it now. Must have been quite a commotion in the car."

"Just about caused me to wreck," Rosie replied. "But I managed to get the car to the shoulder. Fortunately, Badass passed out from the pain, so I was able to get the cuffs on him without a problem."

"Damn pussy cat," Badass said. "That's twice today she's ruined my plans."

"I thought you might have had something to do with Bennie's little exercise this morning," Bert replied. "I'm going to have to recommend Preacher Puss for some kind of special law enforcement award."

"I'd like to wring her neck," Badass replied.

"Well, you won't be doing any of that," Rosie said. "Start marching, you know the way to the cell. I seriously doubt ole Santa Claus will be visiting you tonight. You'll spend Christmas and Monday in jail, and then go before Judge

Oakes on Tuesday morning, since Monday's a holiday. Merry Christmas, Badass!"

After locking Badass in jail, Rosie came back into Bert's office and said, "Well, everything is secure. Someone will have to come back in tomorrow and Monday to feed Badass. I can do that if you wish."

"No, no, Rosie, I'll handle that. You just plan on enjoying Christmas day. I'm sorry you had the problem."

"No problem for me. Ole Preacher Puss took care of everything. I better get back to the car now to make sure she's okay. When I left her she was napping. See you at the party tonight."

"See you," Bert said as he returned to his office.

Chapter 15

Harlan County, Kentucky
December 24

Mrs. Cavanaugh looked approvingly at Fatso and said, "Fatso, or should I say Santa, you look great. You'll be the hit of the party."

Fatso had decided that he would dress in his new Santa outfit before he left work. That way he wouldn't have to worry about changing clothes when he got to the Slusher farm. It was almost 5 pm and he had just changed into the outfit when, as luck would have it, Mrs. Cavanaugh showed up to get a few groceries. She was delighted to see him in the new outfit she had made for him, and she ran around behind the check-out counter to carefully examine it.

"You kept it nicely folded. It doesn't have any bad wrinkles," she said. "You be real sure to be careful on your ride over to the farm. I want you to make a real good impression in the suit I made for you.”

“Yes, Mrs. Cavanaugh,” Fatso replied. “I'll be careful. What's big as an elephant and weighs nothing, Mrs. Cavanaugh?”

She tilted her head and smiled at Fatso.

He said, “An elephant's shadow!”

“It seems strange for Santa Claus to be telling elephant jokes,” Mrs. Cavanaugh said. “I just can't get over what a nice Santa you made, Fatso. Your outfit really looks good. I love your black boots, your hat, and your big beard is just perfect. You look like you just blew in from the North Pole! But where's your gift bag?”

Fatso reached down under the counter and pulled out the large red gift bag and flipped it over his shoulder.

“Ahh,” said Mrs. Cavanaugh. “Now you look perfect. Now you just stand there a minute. I want to get my cell phone and take a picture of you.”

Fatso looked at his watch, and said, “Hurry up, Mrs. Cavanaugh. It's after closing time and I know you still haven't picked out your groceries. I have to get out of here. You wouldn't want to hold up ole Santa would you?”

She held up her cell phone and pressed the button. “Now I've got your picture, Santa. It'll just take me a second to grab my groceries.” She put her phone back in her purse and turned with a grocery basket and headed toward the groceries. “I'll just be a second.”

“Well, hurry up,” replied Fatso.

After about 5 minutes she reappeared at the check out

counter with several groceries in her basket. "Okay, Fatso. Get these checked out and we'll both be gone."

Fatso rang-up the groceries and said, "That'll be Eight dollars and twenty three cents, Mrs. Cavanaugh."

She paid him, gathered her groceries in the bag Fatso had loaded, and turned to walk out of the store. Just as she turned she ran into Trigger Green, who said, "Good afternoon Mrs. Cavanaugh, so good to see you."

"Oh, hi Mr. Green," she said. "Good to see you too." She left the store.

"Fatso, you're running late. I'm not paying you overtime," Trigger said. "You sure do make a good Santa. That's a real handsome outfit."

"Thanks boss," Fatso replied. "Mrs. Cavanaugh just had to show up at closing time and then check out my outfit. And then she had a little shopping to do. So that's why I'm running a little late. But I'm okay, I'm not suppose to get to the party until 6, and it's only 5:15. I'll still get there early. I'm out of here."

"Well, you have a great party. And tell everyone hello and Merry Christmas for me," Trigger replied. "You got Mr. Chang's gift, I hope."

"Sure do, boss, it's right here in my gift bag." Fatso walked from behind the checkout counter and started toward the door. "You have a real good Christmas. Do you know why elephants wear sun glasses?"

"So no one will recognize them," said Trigger with a smile. "That's a really old one."

George answered the intercom at the Slusher brothers' farm gate, "Yes sir?"

"Hi George," Gunsmoke said. "I just wanted to double-check to make sure you had the list of all our expected guests."

"Got it right here on my desk," George replied. "I'll be real anxious for all of them to get here. Then I'll lock up and head up there to join the party!"

"And in addition to the people we're expecting Preacher Puss," chuckled Gunsmoke.

"Yeah, you're right." George said. "I'm sure looking forward to seeing her. It's starting to snow a little....beginning to look a lot like Christmas"

"Just what we ordered," said Gunsmoke. "See you when all the guests have arrived."

"Roger that, boss," answered George. Just as he hung-up the intercom phone two cars approached the gate. George saw who was driving the first and opened the gate. He stuck his head out the guard-house window and shouted, "Merry Christmas, Mr. Richenberger, go right on in. You're the first to arrive. I know Gunsmoke and Booger will be delighted to see you. Hope you had a good trip from Knoxville."

Gus Richenberger shouted back, "Sure did George....little snow on the road now, but not too bad. See you in a bit for the party!" Gus drove on through the gate and it closed behind him.

The next car pulled up and George shouted, "You're a little early Santa. You're not due until midnight!"

Fatso laughed and said, "Ho Ho Ho, George. You either open that gate or I'll bring you a lump of coal!"

"The gate is opening. I'll expect everything I ordered from you, Santa." George joked.

Fatso drove through the gate and on to the house.

George looked at his watch....6:20 pm. He sat back in his chair, closed his eyes, and started dreaming about Christmastime when he was a child. He heard the squeal of brakes and opened his eyes to see a large white van parked at the gate. The lettering on the side of the van said *Grandma's Cookin*. He stood, opened the gatehouse door, and walked outside. The driver of the van had his window rolled down and said, "Got a delivery here for the Slusher boys, George."

"Yeah," George said. "I can smell it, and it smells great! I just need to look in the van, Bobby, if you don't mind."

"Sure thing, George," the driver said as he opened his door and got out of the van. He walked around back and opened the rear doors for George's inspection.

George looked inside and said, "I don't see Grandma in there. Everything looks in order. You go right on up to the house. Drive around to the back entrance. I'll call Booger and tell him you're on the way and he'll meet you back there."

"Will do," the caterer said. "Thanks George, you have a Merry Christmas."

The farm house looked like a picture from Currier and Ives. The snow was gently falling, big white flakes. The ground was partially covered. Approaching the house the driver could see smoke rising from the chimney, and lights shining brightly in every window. He could see a large, fully decorated Christmas tree in the window of their great room. It was covered with multi-colored lights, artificial snow and icicles, and ornaments. There was a large angel perched on top. Beautiful green Christmas wreaths hung on the door and in each window.

Gus Richenberger had just arrived at the farm house. Gunsmoke and Booger had greeted him and invited him to come into the great room and have a seat. "We've got some real good hot cider, Gus," Gunsmoke said.

"Oh boy, that sounds terrific. It would hit the spot," Gus replied.

All six of the North Koreans were already seated in the great room, three on one side of the large fireplace and three on the other. Each Korean had a cat in their lap watching intently everything that was going on. A huge fire was burning with a pleasant smell and crackling embers. Charlie and Ray were standing beside the beautiful Christmas tree chatting. Gus had shaken hands and greeted each upon his arrival.

Booger handed Gus a cup of cider and said, "Take a seat anywhere. You're the first arrival, we're expecting 9 others before we get underway around 7."

"Thanks," Gus said to Booger as he took a seat with his cider.

Booger's cell phone vibrated in his pocket. He pulled it out and answered it, saying, "Okay George, I'll head to the back door to meet him and we'll get the food all set up. Thanks. Bye bye." Booger then walked over to Gunsmoke and said,

"Brother, the caterer just got here. I'm going to meet him and get the food set up. You cover the front door."

"Sure will," Gunsmoke replied as his brother went trotting off toward the kitchen and back of the house.

The doorbell rang.

Gunsmoke opened the door and got a huge smile on his face as he said, "Ho Ho Ho, if it isn't the grand ole man himself. Welcome to our humble home, Santa. Since you're here, I guess that means we've all been good this year!"

"Don't know that I'd go that far," replied Fatso, aka Santa, as he grinned and said "but I did decide to stop by for a visit, if that's okay?" He sat his Santa bag down beside the door.

"No one could be more welcome, my friend. Do come in," Gunsmoke replied.

As Santa and Gunsmoke walked into the great room all six of the Koreans shouted in unison "Mr. Fatso Santa..... Merry Christmas!". They jumped up from their seats and the cats went flying from their laps. They ran over to Fatso and started shaking his hand and slapping his back. General O said, "Mr. Fatso, how about you tell us a joke. We love to hear them."

Fatso grinned and said, "You know what's blue and has big ears?"

The six looked intently with anticipatory grins and shook their heads.

"An elephant at the North Pole!" Fatso replied.

The Koreans, laughing loudly, started to clap their hands and again slap Fatso on his back.

Fatso then walked around the room and greeted the

others already there. He stood with Charlie and Ray chatting beside the Christmas tree.

The doorbell rang again.

When Gunsmoke opened the door he was delighted to see Pastor Raymond Bell and his wife Betty, Sheriff J. Bert Sterling, and Carolyn and Kyle Potter. He welcomed each of them with handshakes and hugs, and then ushered them into the great room to meet and greet the others. They all took seats and Gunsmoke served them hot cider.

Two more cars pulled up to the gate, one behind the other. Mayor Fred Knapp rolled down his car window and shouted, "Hey George, it's me....ole Fred."

George opened the window of his guard house and shouted back at Fred, "Merry Christmas Mayor Knapp. Lovely evening for a Christmas party! You go right on in, and I'll be up in a little while to join you."

"Thanks, George!" The gate swung open and Fred drove through.

The next car behind pulled up to the gate house and stopped. Rosie Cain rolled down her window and said, "Hi George. Rosie Cain and Preacher Puss reporting in!"

George closed his guard house window, opened its door and walked outside to Rosie's car. He saw Preacher Puss sitting in the passenger seat and said, "Rosie it's just great to see you and that cat. You think she might let me give her a pet?"

"Well, I don't know," Rosie replied. "You don't have any Whisker Lickins, but she might agree, since its Christmas eve and all." Rosie then reached over and lifted Preacher Puss up toward her window.

George put a hand in, stroked the cat several times, and said, "Preacher Puss, Merry Christmas. I hope ole Santa brings you a nice, big, juicy mouse."

"Bad," replied Rosie with a chuckle as she returned the cat to his seat. "Preacher Puss is very, very particular what she eats. She does not eat mice."

"You two go right on in, I know everyone's anxious to see you," George said as he removed the remote control from his coat pocket and pressed the button to open the gate.

Rosie and Preacher Puss drove through.

George returned inside the gate house and took a seat at his desk. He looked over the guest list and noticed that the only person yet to arrive was Dr. Randy Peters. He looked at his watch. It was almost 7 o'clock. The snow was picking up a bit. He reached for the thermos sitting on his desk, removed the cap, and poured a steaming cup of coffee. He sat back in his chair, propped his feet up on the desk, and started sipping the warm liquid.

After finishing about half the cup he saw headlights in the distance coming up the road. He put down his feet and coffee and opened his window.

Dr. Randy Peters stopped at the guard gate, rolled down his window, and shouted, "Did you order this snow, George?"

George replied, "Nope, but it sure is pretty. Good to see you made it Dr. Peters. You're the last to arrive. Merry Christmas to you. I'll open the gate, you go right on to the house. I'm not far behind you."

"Thanks George," Randy said. "I'll see you there."

Gunsmoke answered the intercom, "Yes, George?"

"Hey, boss," said George. "All guests have reported. Dr. Peters is on his way. I'm going to lock up and head up there if that's okay with you."

"Great! I was beginning to get a little worried about Randy. I'm glad he made it safely. You get on up here."

"Will do, thanks," George said.

Mayor Knapp had arrived and joined the group, and just as Gunsmoke was announcing the mayor the doorbell rung again. When he opened the door he saw a smiling Rosie Cain holding a bright-eyed Preacher Puss. As soon as all in the great room saw the two of them they jumped up and rushed over to greet them. As the Koreans jumped out of their seats their cats once again went flying out of their laps, and this immediately caught the attention of Preacher Puss. She started swishing her tail, squirming, and meowing, indicating to Rosie that she wanted down to visit with her fellow felines. A great sniffing and hissing encounter followed, but all the cats seemed to accept Preacher Puss warmly. The Koreans lined up to each give Preacher Puss kind words and pets. She was the center of attention for the moment. Eventually everyone again took a seat and continued conversations.

Gunsmoke stood at the entrance to the great room and announced, "Friends, our last guest has now arrived.....Randy Peters."

"Merry Christmas to all," Randy said loudly. "The snow got a little heavier as I got into the mountains of Eastern Kentucky. So my trip from Lexington took a little longer than usual. But it went well, and I'm so glad to see each of you.

I'm thankful that I can share Christmas eve with all my dear friends."

"Here, here," said Mayor Knapp. "Come in and have a cup of cider, Dr. Peters."

Randy walked around the room greeting all his friends. When he came to Pastor Raymond and Betty Bell he said, "I sure appreciate you two allowing me to spend the night with you this evening. With this snow the drive back to Lexington could have been a bit touchy."

"No problem whatsoever," Betty Bell said. "We're honored to have you stay with us."

Gus Richenberger was seated beside the Bells and overheard their conversation with Randy. He said, "Yeah, I'm a little concerned with my drive back to Knoxville tonight, but since that's going south rather than north maybe I'll be okay."

Booger Slusher had just returned to the great room from assisting the caterer get the food arranged when he heard what Gus said and replied, "Hey Gus, you know you're more than welcome to stay over with us. We got plenty of room."

"Thanks for the offer, Booger," Gus said. "But I've got family back in Knoxville to spend Christmas day with. I'm sure I won't have any trouble driving. My car's got four wheel drive."

Just then George walked into the great room with Gunsmoke who clapped his hands loudly to get his guests' attention and said, "My good friends, with the arrival just now of George we now have all 21 people and a whole bunch of cats ready to celebrate Christmas eve. Booger and I feel very, very blessed to have such fine friends, and we sincerely thank each of you for spending your Christmas eve with us. We hope we can make it enjoyable for you. It is now just a little past 7 pm, so I think it's about time for our dinner. If you would, please join me in the dining room for the blessing by Pastor Bell and then our meal."

Everyone burst into applause with a lot of smiles and nodding heads as they proceeded to the dining room.

The table was beautifully set. The catered meals were on the table, and holiday decorations in red and green were sitting on a spotless, white table cloth. Gunsmoke sat at one end of the table, Booger at the other. Fatso, aka Santa Claus, sat in the middle of one side, and Pastor Raymond and Betty Bell sat in the middle of the other side. After all had found their places, Gunsmoke stood and said, "My friends, God has blessed us bountifully. I would now ask Pastor Bell if he would be so kind as to lead us in a prayer of thanksgiving."

Raymond then stood, asked all to bow their heads, and said, "Heavenly Father, we thank thee for allowing us to gather this day before Christmas with friends to celebrate the birth of our savior, Jesus Christ. We are so thankful for the gift that he gave to us, eternal life for all who would believe and accept. We thank you for the tremendous blessings you have bestowed upon us. And now we ask your blessing on this food. Bless it to the use of our bodies, and us to Thy service. Amen."

A resounding 'Amen' was heard throughout the room, and then each began to enjoy the meal along with the fellowship of all those present.

After eating the meal, Gunsmoke and Booger served a delicious ice cream sundae they had put together for a dessert. The ice cream was a dark green lime with a bright red strawberry sitting on top. Around the strawberry was a circle of white whipped cream. Sugared sparkles of various colors were sprinkled on top. Coffee accompanied the dessert.

Once everyone had finished their treat, Gunsmoke again rose and said, "I hope everyone enjoyed the meal. I know you enjoyed visiting with all your friends. I thought now would be a good time for us to adjourn back to the great room. I think ole Santa wants to distribute some gifts."

The group gradually left the dining room, with most patting their stomachs and saying what a wonderful meal they had just consumed.

Booger grabbed Fatso and said, "Hey Santa, let's go in the study to fill your gift bag." The two of them walked together.

Fatso said, "Booger, I need to grab my bag....I left it beside the front door."

After retrieving his gift bag, with one gift already inside, Fatso and Booger walked to the study. Inside was a large stack of beautifully wrapped Christmas gifts sitting on a table beside the wall. Fatso said, "Do I put all those gifts in my bag?"

"That's the idea," Booger replied. "Gunsmoke and I purchased a gift for everyone attending this evening. Plus, there are other gifts, too, from the Koreans and from Charlie, George, and Ray. You think your bag's going to hold them all?"

"Now Booger, you know that ole Santa can accommodate any number of gifts. I'll get 'em all in the bag....don't you worry."

Fatso started stuffing all the presents into his gift bag. It started to bulge, but he managed to get them all in. The two then left the study headed back to the great room.

Gunsmoke had started playing Christmas music over the sound system. Several more logs were added to the roaring fire. All assembled in the great room were enjoying chatting with each other and petting cats.....particularly Preacher Puss.

When Fatso appeared at the entrance with his enormous gift bag held over one shoulder Booger shouted loudly, "Okay everybody, please take your seats. Santa just got here from the North Pole and, as you can see, he has brought numerous gifts, many of which have your names on them. So if you will continue to be good little boys and girls and quietly have a seat, I'll bet he might start to distribute the presents."

The group then quietly took their seats. But before Santa began distributing his gifts Randy Peters stood and said, "Friends, could I have your attention for just a moment before Santa does his thing." He then reached up behind his neck and pulled the necklace he was wearing over his head. When he did, the astoundingly beautiful golden Seibert anchor cross attached to the necklace came out from under his sweater. Everyone in the room let out an audible gasp. Light reflecting off the artifact scattered throughout the room. Total silence followed. Everyone was staring at the anchor cross.

"I think everyone knows that this is the Seibert anchor cross," he said as he held it in his right hand. "I also think that everyone here is aware that General O has been selected to go on a very, very important and perilous mission. When he was approached for this mission by our country's intelligence community he readily accepted, knowing full well about how important and dangerous it was. His only request was for the agents to inquire to see if he might be able to wear one of the anchor crosses on his journey. As you are aware, all the owners of the anchor crosses live outside the United States except for one." Dr. Peters then pointed his finger toward Kyle Potter. "Deputy Potter owns this Seibert anchor cross. After getting the request from Agent Clair Eaton I phoned Kyle to see if he would agree to let General O borrow it while he's gone on his mission. Kyle readily agreed. So I brought it here tonight to present to General O. I must add that I think it very appropriate and fitting that it be given as a temporary gift on this, the eve of celebrating the birth of Jesus Christ. It was He who blessed the very gold from which this anchor cross is made. What could be more appropriate than to now present it to General O to wear as he goes on his important mission for the United States."

Dr. Randy Peters then walked to the chair where General O sat, and said, "General, I know I speak on behalf of every person here in this room, and for many, many more not with us tonight, when I say thank you so very much for your willingness to serve your new country." Randy then placed the necklace with the Seibert anchor cross around General O's neck. "This beautiful artifact is known to possess mysterious and wonderful powers to protect from harm those who wear it for peaceful purposes. May the Lord go with you."

The room burst into applause. When it subsided General O spoke, "Dr. Peters, Deputy Potter, and all my other wonderful friends, it is an honor for me to have been chosen for my upcoming mission. I am so pleased to have been asked to serve my new country. I only hope and pray that I do not fail, and I feel certain that this Seibert anchor cross will help me be successful. Merry Christmas to each of you."

Another thunderous round of applause came from all in the room. Santa then walked to the center of the room and sat his gift bag in front of him. He then asked Gunsmoke and Booger if they would assist him in distributing the gifts. The two brothers, Gunsmoke dressed in a bright green shirt and Booger wearing a bright red, walked over beside Santa and blended in with his outfit perfectly.

Gunsmoke said, "Okay, Santa, we're here to play Santa's helpers." Booger nodded in agreement and smiled. The room grew silent.

Fatso reached down and pulled out the first gift on the top, read the label, and handed the gift to Gunsmoke as he said, "First gift goes to Betty Bell." Gunsmoke then delivered the gift to Betty, and she started opening it.

The process was repeated many times over the next 30 or so minutes until everyone in the room had gifts and wrapping paper all around them. All the friends were talking with each other, showing their gifts, and enjoying looking at those of others.

Fatso then said loudly to all, "Well, well, I think ole Santa's finally reached the bottom of his gift bag." He reached in the bottom and pulled out a gift about the size of a shoe box wrapped in metallic green paper with a big red bow. He looked at the card attached to the top of the gift and said, "To Choe Yong-ho."

Booger took the gift, walked over to where Choe was seated, and handed it to him. Choe looked amazed at the beautiful present. He carefully started to unwrap it.

Sitting on Choe's right was Deputy Rosie Cain. Rosie had just been honored by Preacher Puss when she came over and jumped back into Rosie's lap after visiting around the room. Rosie reached in a pocket and pulled out two Whisker Lickin treats and gave them to the cat. Preacher Puss was licking her chops and gently swishing her tail.

Immediately on Choe's left was seated Dr. Randy Peters. Randy was talking with General O, who was seated on Randy's left.....two seats over from Choe. General O was holding and carefully examining the Seibert anchor cross that hung about his neck as Randy discussed its history with him.

Choe finished removing all the wrapping paper from his gift. There was a lid on the top of the boxed gift. His right hand now rested on the lid as he prepared to lift it.

Suddenly General O, holding the anchor cross, said to Dr. Peters, "This anchor cross is feeling really hot."

The color drained from Randy's face as he reached and felt the artifact.

At the same time Preacher Puss turned her head and looked straight at the gift in Choe's hand. She then leaped out of Rosie's lap and landed atop Choe's right hand that was about to lift the lid. Her claws were extended and dug into his hand. Choe screamed in pain, and instinctively lifted the hand up and backwards to try and shake off the cat. Preacher Puss retracted her claws and fell to the floor.

Randy immediately reached over and placed his hand atop the gift box in Choe's lap. He said, "We've got a problem, Choe. Don't open that box."

Sheriff Sterling ran over to Choe and said to Randy, "What's wrong?"

Randy replied, "Not sure Bert, but we've gotten every indication that there's a problem with Choe's gift. When Choe was about to open it the anchor cross heated up as it always does when danger is imminent for the person wearing it, and Preacher Puss seemed to sense something and jumped on Choe's hand preventing him from lifting the lid. I've got to believe that the gift is not what it appears to be."

"I see," the sheriff replied. He carefully reached down and lifted the gift off of Choe's lap. He then looked over at Deputy Kyle Potter and said, "Kyle, help me here. Go open the front door."

Kyle walked rapidly in front of Bert toward the door. Kyle opened the door and Bert walked outside, carefully holding the box in front of him. He walked across the driveway and another hundred yards to the tree line. He sat the box down on the ground. "Kyle, jump in my cruiser and call the state police. Tell them to send the bomb squad here, I want that box x-rayed and evaluated."

"Will do," said Kyle as he started running toward Bert's cruiser that Rosie had parked a short distance away.

Bert then walked back to the house. Many of the guest had gathered at the front door to watch what was going on.

He told them to go back into the great room and have a seat. When they all were settled and Kyle had returned, Bert said, "Folks, I don't know what kind of problem we have here, or even if we have a problem. But as Dr. Peters said, we had strong indications that Choe's gift was bogus. So we're going to check it out. The state police are on their way. They'll x-ray the package and determine what's inside. I've got it a safe distance from the house, so you are in no danger. Let's just continue to enjoy our evening as best we can, and after the state police check out the box I'll let you know the results."

George grabbed his coat and said to Bert as he headed to the door, "I'll go back down to the gate to let the police in when they get here."

"Thanks, George," Bert said. "Sorry to cause you that trouble."

"No problem," George replied as he left the house.

Only a few minutes passed after George unlocked the gatehouse door and went inside until he could hear a siren in the distance. It kept getting louder, and then a state police van appeared coming up the driveway with its emergency lights flashing and siren sounding. George hit the button to open the gate. The van driver stuck his head out when beside the gatehouse and said, "Where's the sheriff?"

"Straight ahead," George replied. "You can't miss him!"

The van accelerated through the gate.

The sheriff and his chief deputy were standing in the driveway in front of the home as the van arrived. The driver and another officer got out of the van and walked over to Bert and Kyle.

Bert said, "You guys got here fast. The package is right over there." Bert pointed toward the box, now almost covered with snow.

The two state policemen then opened the back of the van and grabbed bomb suits. After putting them on they got a case that contained a mobile x-ray unit and started walking toward the suspicious box. They looked like two Pillsbury doughboys. Once at the target they assembled the mobile x-ray unit beside it, and then carefully lifted the box and placed it in the unit. Bert and Kyle watched them from the front of the house. Fortunately, there was enough light coming from the house to allow the state policemen to see. After another five minutes of manipulating the x-ray unit, the two left it and walked back over to the sheriff.

"You guys sure did the right thing," said state policeman #1. "That thing's a bomb for sure. It looks like 4 pipe bombs rigged to be triggered when the box lid is opened. We could see the wires from the detonator running to the lid. If it had been opened inside everyone in the room would have been killed. We're going to back our van over to it and load it in a bomb box to transport. We'll take it to Post 10 and it'll then go to our Frankfort lab for analysis and destruction. I'll make sure you get the report as soon as we have it. In the meantime, you have a great Christmas and thank the good Lord for His watching over everyone!"

Bert and Kyle shook hands with both policemen. Bert said to them, "Really appreciate it guys. Not a good way for you to spend Christmas eve, but we're awfully grateful. Take care, and I'll look to get the report when you have it."

The two got in the van and drove it over beside the box's location. They removed the bomb from the x-ray unit and placed it carefully in the bomb box in their van. They packed up the portable x-ray unit and then headed back to Post 10.

Bert and Kyle walked back into the house, and after shaking off the accumulated snow from their jackets they removed them, hung them up, and walked back into the great room where all the guests were engaged in muted conversation. When they saw the two they all became silent and looked expectantly.

Bert walked to the center of the room and said, "It was a bomb. Had the lid been removed we would all not lived to see Christmas. The bomb squad x-rayed the box and could clearly determine it contained four pipe bombs that would have been detonated by removing the lid. That's all we really know presently. The device will be sent to Frankfort for a full analysis, and I'll get a report once that's done. Two things happened tonight that saved our lives. One was the Seibert anchor cross. It started to heat up, and fortunately Dr. Peters knew that was a sign that the person wearing it, in this case General O, was in danger. The second thing that happened was that Preacher Puss somehow sensed the pending danger and jumped on Choe's hand that was getting ready to lift the lid. We really don't understand either of these two things.... we just know they happened. The thing with the anchor cross follows a long list of similar occurrences involving the artifacts, but we still really don't fully understand why or how it happens. And how Preacher Puss could have sensed the impending danger....well, we'll never understand that. But she did. Maybe it's a thing like when animals have been known to sense earthquakes before they happen. I don't know. I do know we should be very, very grateful. We came extremely close this evening to exiting the world of the living. Remember that in your prayers tonight."

All began then to say their good byes to the Slusher brothers, and to thank them for the wonderful evening. And it had been, except for the ending.

Bert walked over to Fatso who was sitting by himself in a corner of the room. "Hey Santa, that last gift was a real dozy. You got any idea where it came from?"

Fatso looked up at the sheriff and said, "Yeah, I know exactly where it came from." He went on to relate to Bert how a stranger had arranged for him to deliver the gift to Choe, saying that the stranger, a Mr. Wong Chang, said he had been hired by Choe's parents to try and convince him to return home to North Korea. He claimed the present had a gift in it and a card asking Choe to call him so they could talk. And he said it had to be kept a secret."

"Trigger and I didn't see anything wrong with delivering the gift, Bert," Fatso said. "We'll cooperate fully with you to try and get that crook. He almost killed us all!"

"Thanks, Fatso," Bert said. "I know you and Trigger couldn't have had knowledge about the bomb. I'll drop by later to talk about it. You have a great Christmas."

Randy Peters stood talking with General O. Bert walked up to the pair and said, "Guys, once again the power of that anchor cross has been demonstrated. General O, that little demonstration should make you feel a lot safer about your upcoming mission."

General O said, "Yes sir. I do indeed feel much better and safer about it."

Randy then said, "You know, I'm sure glad Preacher Puss did what he did to stop Choe from opening the lid, but it would be my opinion that if the lid had been opened the bomb would not have detonated. The anchor cross would have prevented it....somehow....someway. And like you said, Bert, we still don't understand it, but we do know it's protective power has been demonstrated many times."

Bert nodded his head in approval, and then looked over at Rosie, still sitting in her chair with Preacher Puss back in her lap. Bert said, "Rosie, you give that cat an extra helping of Whisker Lickins. She's sure earned them." He then reached down and gave the cat a nice pet. Preacher Puss meowed loudly. She then laid her head back down and continued her nap.

Chapter 16

Knoxville, Tennessee
December 25

General Park, aka Wong Chang, woke up Christmas morning with a terrible headache. He had hardly slept. How could his plan have not worked? He had arrived yesterday at the home of Pretty Boy Maggard and the two of them celebrated last night, anticipating a lead story about the bomb explosion on the 11 o'clock television news. There was none. About half way through the program there was a story from Harlan about the Kentucky State Police bomb squad removing an unexploded device from a Harlan county farm. He had failed. He knew sudden death would await him when he arrived back home. At midnight he called Kim Jung-un and reported that the bomb had apparently failed to detonate. The Supreme Leader turned the air blue with shouting, curses, and threats about the ways he would be tortured before dying. After about 15 minutes he calmed down enough for General Park to say that he would go back to Harlan on Monday and devise another plan that would accomplish the goal. Kim's response and final words before he slammed down his phone were, "You damn well better come up with something to eliminate them all, or else just eliminate yourself."

General Park and Pretty Boy Maggard were sitting at the kitchen table drinking coffee. Both looked very tired and exhausted. Pretty Boy said, "General, I don't know anything about that bomb thing, except it didn't work. I sure hope you've got a plan B."

General Park responded, "I'm working on plan B. I'll get something figured out today, and drive back to Harlan early in the morning. After I accomplish my mission there, I'll come back here to fly home."

"That's going to cost some extra money. This extension wasn't a part of the deal for me. I'll need an additional $10,000."

"You'll get it, when I come back. If I don't succeed I won't be back and you'll not be earning the money," General Park said.

Pretty Boy looked over at General Park, smiled, and said, "Merry Christmas, General."

Harlan, Kentucky

The morning worship service at New Hope Baptist Church was packed to capacity. Christmas came on a Sunday this year. Pastor Raymond Bell had just finished a very meaningful sermon, and he was greeting his parishioners as they left the church. During his sermon he had discussed the events that occurred at the Slusher brothers' farm the previous evening, and had described how he thought the Lord had intervened to protect them. The congregation listened intently to his every word. They had all just heard rumors about what had happened last night, and were delighted to learn the facts and details.

Pastor Bell extended his hand to Carolyn Potter as she exited the church escorted by Sheriff J. Bert Sterling. The pastor said, "I could hardly sleep last night, I hope my message this morning was appropriate."

Carolyn said, "Raymond, it could not have been more appropriate. Thank you for sharing it with the congregation."

Bert nodded in approval as he shook the pastor's hand and said, "Ditto that, my friend."

Raymond asked, "Have any idea how long it will be before getting the report from the state police?"

Bert shook his head negatively and said, "Not really, but likely about the middle of the week."

Carolyn and Bert walked down the church steps, and Raymond continued greeting his parishioners.

The last two people out of the church were Betty Bell

and Dr. Randy Peters. The two had been chatting until Raymond finished greeting his flock. They walked up to him, and Randy said, "Pastor, it was certainly a most interesting trip for me. The party last night was just excellent, despite the disturbance at the end. And the good Lord did protect us all. And then the hospitality you and Betty provided for me could not have been better. Thank you so much for that, and for the excellent service and sermon at your church this morning."

Betty replied, "We enjoyed so much having you stay with us Randy. Anytime you're in Harlan you're most welcome in our home."

Raymond added, "Betty said it well, my friend. And you have a good and safe drive back to Lexington. Remember, you don't have that Seibert anchor cross to protect you going home."

Randy laughed and said, "Yeah, Raymond, you're right. I guess I'm on my own!"

———

General O was in his room packing for his trip. He sat down on the bed beside his suitcase. The Seibert anchor cross remained on the necklace about his neck. He had not removed it since putting it on last night. He lifted it up with his right hand and looked at it with great admiration. It gave him a definite sense of security. He reread the words across the horizontal arm of the cross, **Pax Tecum**. He knew they were latin and meant 'Peace be with you'. He just hoped that would be the case. He released the anchor cross and it fell tight on the necklace. He looked at his left wrist and the new watch he had been given. A chill went up his spine when he thought about the fact that while onboard the ship if he pressed the cap on the back of the watch three quick times it would be the end of him and all on the boat. He prayed that it would never come to that. He thought about how marvelous the technology that enabled the microphone in his watch to pick up all sound and transmit it to friendly forces that would be monitoring. He finished packing all his clothes, closed his suitcase, and sat it on the floor. It was natural to be afraid, he thought. Indeed this could be his final journey. He tried to put those thoughts out of his mind and dwell on positive things. This was his great opportunity to be of service to his new country, which had been so very good to him and his five cohorts. The Slusher brothers and all the other new friends had been very special. He would accomplish this mission successfully, and would look forward to returning here to live out his life with all his friends.

Chapter 17

Knoxville, Tennessee
December 26

Pretty Boy Maggard said, "General, I hope you have better luck this trip. From what you've told me your boss ain't gonna tolerate much more. He sounds like a real ass."

General Park replied, "Yeah, it's pretty much his way or you're dead. I'm going to try real hard this trip to make it go to suit him."

The two men were standing in Pretty Boy Maggard's driveway. Pretty Boy had gotten the general another rental car, so the old one wouldn't be recognized in Harlan. The two shook hands and General Park got in his car and drove off.

Harlan County, Kentucky

"Fatso, I still can't believe what happened at that Party Saturday night," Trigger Green said. He was standing in front of the check-out counter. Fatso had called him as soon as he got home after the party and told him what happened.

"Yeah, I can associate with that," Fatso replied. "We came about as close as you can to all being killed. I sure hope they catch that Wong Chang, or whatever his real name is. That SOB just about blew us all up."

Trigger said, "Well, unfortunately, he's likely back home by now. I got paid handsomely from him, but if I'd known what he was planning I would have stuck that money up his ass and kicked him out of here. Not only was he trying to kill that Choe fellow, but he knew it'd also get you and all those others. My blood pressure goes up 50 points just thinking about it."

"Hey Trigger, you know what's grey with red spots?" Fatso asked.

"An elephant with measles," Trigger replied. "That one's old as the hills. I believe you're slipping, Fatso. You need some new material."

"An oldie, but goodie," Fatso replied.

Trigger turned and walked back to his office.

Fatso turned and looked out the grocery store window just in time to see a black, government-looking car pass by with three occupants. He picked up the book he was reading, leaned back in his chair, put his feet up on the counter, closed his eyes and dozed off.

Claiborne County, Tennessee

General Park had left Knoxville on highway 33 to Tazewell where he turned onto highway 32 going toward Cumberland Gap where he'd pick up 25E to Pineville, Kentucky, and from there travel on highway 119 to Harlan. It was a two and one half hour trip.

He had been racking his brain to come up with a plan to eliminate the deserters. He knew he couldn't get any help from Trigger Green, since he'd almost blown up old Fatso. So he'd have to do this pretty much on his own. He wasn't sure how he would do it, but do it he would.

Just as he was about 5 miles north of Tazewell on highway 32 he passed a black, official-looking sedan. Little did he know that in that car was the leader of the deserters he was trying to kill.

General O had been telling agents Clair Eaton and Rose McKay all about the events that had transpired on Saturday night. The general was sitting in the back seat. The two federal agents shook their heads. Agent Eaton said, "If that thing had exploded everything would have been ruined, including you."

"Thankfully it did not," General O replied. He reached down under the sweater he was wearing and rubbed the Seibert anchor cross. "I feel certain that I'll be okay on this mission."

"We're going to have to look into that incident anyway," Agent McKay replied. "For all we know the bomb could have been intended for you. It's scary. Someone definitely wanted one or more of the people at that party eliminated. And the person didn't mind to kill 21 people. We'll report it back to our people, and wheels will start to move to identify and capture whoever was responsible."

"That would be good," the general replied.

The car continued its journey toward the Knoxville airport.

Harlan, Kentucky

It was mid afternoon. Many of the stores in Harlan closed for the holidays between Christmas and New Years. Creech Cafe did not. Fred had opened the store on its regular schedule this morning. Sheriff Sterling, Deputy Potter, and Raymond Bell were all sitting at a table enjoying coffee and a piece of Fred's good apple pie. Fred walked over, pulled up a chair, and joined them.

"Boys, it's going to take a while to get over Saturday night. I had nightmares about it for the last two nights." the Mayor said.

"All's well that ends well," Kyle replied, "and it certainly did end well!"

"Amen," Raymond Bell affirmed.

The sheriff said, "I'll feel a whole lot better about the whole thing if we can catch that Wong Chang person. I've talked with both Fatso and Trigger Green about him, and got a good description. The state police will likely send an artist over to Maggard's grocery and make a sketch of him from Fatso and Trigger's descriptions. If he hasn't left the country, I think we'll eventually nail him."

Raymond was down to the last bite of his apple pie when Polly flew over and landed on his shoulder. "Polly hungry. Polly hungry," she said. Raymond reached down and stuck his fork in the small piece of pie and held it up to Polly. She gobbled it down in one bite. "Thank you. Thank you," she said as she flew back to her perch. Raymond said, "You are most welcome my friend."

Fred smiled and said, "I'll take that off your bill, Raymond."

"No, no. I enjoyed it. Me and ole Polly are good friends," Raymond said.

All four men turned when they heard a roar of laughter from the back of the store. They saw old Bobby bent over laughing after reading one of Fred's wall postings. Fred said, "Well, I guess I'd better go see what Bobby thinks is so funny." He stood and walked toward his friend.

"Hey Bobby, something tickle your funny bone?" Fred asked.

Bobby pointed toward an article from the **Harlan Daily Enterprise** that Fred had cut out and taped to the wall recently.

Fred looked at it, grinned, and said, "Oh yeah, that is a good one."

The article read:

Several men were in the locker room of a golf club. A cellular phone on a bench rings and a man engages the speaker phone and begins to talk. Everyone else listens.

Man: "Hello"

Woman: "Hi honey, it's me. You at the club?"

Man: "Yep"

Woman: "I'm at the shop and just found this beautiful new leather coat. It's only $2,000. Is it okay if I buy it?

Man: "Sure, go ahead if you like it that much."

Woman: "I also stopped by the Lexus dealership and saw the new models. I saw one I really liked."

Man: "How much?"

Woman: "$90,000."

Man: "Okay, but for that price I hope it's got all the options."

Woman: "Great, one more thing, honey. I was just talking to Minnie and found out that the house I wanted last year is back on the market. They're asking $980,000 for it."

Man: "Well, go ahead and make an offer of $900,000. They'll probably take it. If not, we can go the extra eighty thousand if that's what you want."

Woman: "Thanks honey. See you later. Love you"

Man: "Bye. I love you too."

The man hangs up. The other men in the locker room are staring at him in astonishment, mouths wide open. The man then asks, "Anyone know whose phone this is?"

Bobby slaps Fred on the back and says, "Mr. Mayor, you sure do have a good sense of humor."

Fred walks back to the table and again joins his three friends.

Bert said, "I'm really concerned about General O. The mission he left on this morning sounds like it might really be dangerous. Course I'm just guessing.....the feds didn't tell me anything. But from talking with everyone at the party Saturday night it just seemed like he was going to be at great risk."

Pastor Bell said, "I got that feeling too, Bert, so I think we should all keep him in our prayers."

After their experience on Christmas Eve, the four friends had driven over to the Slusher farm early this morning to see General O off on his journey. Charlie had called Gunsmoke as soon as they arrived at the gate, and Gunsmoke told him to send them on in. Everyone at the farm had gotten up extra early to be part of the send off for General O. A big breakfast was served at 6 am, and then afterwards everyone just sat around the table and continued to drink coffee and chat with General O. They awaited the arrival of Agents Eaton and McKay. Before the feds arrived the four friends joined the others at the table. After another 15 or so minutes the two federal agents arrived at the gate and Charlie called Gunsmoke to announce them. Everyone at the table then grabbed their coats and they all walked outside onto the front porch with General O, Sheriff Sterling carrying his suitcase.

As the dark sedan approached the house Clair Eaton, the driver, said to Rose McKay, "Looks like a big send-off committee."

The car stopped in front of the house. The ladies got out and greeted everyone. Sheriff Sterling put the general's suitcase in the trunk. General O then stood beside the car's rear door and looked back at all his friends standing on the porch and said, "Words fail me. What wonderful friends I'm blessed to have. Thanks to each of you for saying you'll remember me in your prayers. I feel greatly honored to be going on this mission. I'll think of each of you every day, and will look forward greatly to returning soon. May God bless."

General O turned and got in the car's rear seat. The agents got in and drove off to a cheering and waving crowd. The mission had begun.

Chapter 18

Knoxville, Tennessee
December 26

The trip to the Knoxville airport was made without much conversation. General O sat in the backseat deep in thought about his mission. As they approached the McGhee Tyson airport General O noticed that they did not appear to be going to the commercial terminal. He said, "Ladies, am I not going to the terminal?"

Agent Eaton replied, "Not the commercial terminal, General. You have a special ride waiting at the Air National Guard base that adjoins the commercial airport."

After another five minutes they arrived at an entrance gate. A guard came out and walked up to the driver's window. Agent Eaton rolled down her window, flashed her credentials, and said, "Good morning, I'm Agent Clair Eaton. We're making a special delivery for Oak Ridge."

The guard looked carefully at the three in the car, and then pointed to a plane sitting on the tarmac. He said, "That's it over there. I know they're waiting for you." He went back in the guardhouse and pressed a button that opened the gate.

Oak Ridge was the intelligence community's code name for General O's mission. The town of Oak Ridge, Tennessee was only about 40 miles from the Knoxville airport. It was there during the early 1940s that most of the work was performed to develop the first atomic bomb.

As they approached the plane General O's eyes got large as saucers. He said, "I wasn't anticipating this. Are you saying I'm going to be flown in THAT?"

Agent McKay laughed and said, "General O, nothing but the very best for you!. What you're looking at is the latest and greatest in a Gulfstream jet. It's a Gulfstream G650. It cruises at mach 0.85 and has a range of about 7,000 miles. It's powered by two Rolls-Royce BR725 A1-12 engines, and can accommodate up to 19 passengers. Of course on this trip it has a lot fewer, just yourself and a couple of folks to keep you company, plus the crew. I know you'll enjoy the ride!"

Agent Eaton stopped the car beside the sleek aircraft. It had no markings other than tail numbers. Two persons were standing at the foot of the stairs leading into the plane. Both were dressed in suits.

General O and agents Eaton and McKay got out of the car. Agent McKay walked around and retrieved the general's suitcase from the trunk. The two suits got smiles on their faces and extended their hands as the three approached them.

Suit #1 said, "Top of the morning folks. I'm Admiral Jones....just like in John Paul Jones! It's great to see you made the trip okay." The admiral reached and took the suitcase from Agent McKay.

Suit #2 then said, "I'm agent Fong. I too am delighted to see and meet you."

All shook hands, and then entered the plane.

"Well, General O, this is where we part company," said Clair Eaton. "Rose and I will be driving back to Washington. But we'll be paying close attention to your progress. I'm sure the admiral and Agent Fong will keep you entertained on your flight. You have been a delight to work with over these few weeks, and I feel certain that our paths may cross again."

Agent McKay then said, "I ditto that remark, General O. And let me add that I know your mission will go well. You are well prepared, and you have the very best of support. Plus, you are uniquely qualified. All that plus the beautiful, golden anchor cross you're wearing will certainly lead to a successful mission. May God speed."

General O gave big hugs to each of the ladies and said, "You two have been wonderful to work with. And I certainly do feel extremely well prepared, thanks to you." He then patted his sweater on the spot where the anchor cross lay beneath and smiled. "I'm going to be just fine!"

The two ladies departed the jet. The stairs were immediately retracted, and one of the crew members asked the three passengers to please take a seat and prepare for takeoff. There was a round table situated about mid way in the cabin and the admiral indicated for General O to have a seat there. The seats at the table were very similar to the other aircraft seats and had seat belts. Each of the three got belted and the plane began to taxi. Quickly it got airborne.

The crew member, a young man, came into the cabin and asked for drink orders. All requested coffee. It was served and General O said, "This is unreal for me. I was expecting to board a commercial aircraft and be just one of hundreds of passengers."

Admiral Jones said, "General, you are very, very special. Your mission will result in saving the lives of millions of Americans. We are going to do everything in our power to make certain you succeed."

General O said, "I certainly appreciate it. Could you tell me a bit about our schedule?"

The admiral said, "Sure. We must make one stop for fuel. That will be in Los Angeles. It will take us about three and one half hours to get there. Then the flight to Japan will be another 10 hours....we'll cover about 5500 miles on that leg. If everything goes according to plan, we'll arrive at Ishigaki, Japan around 2 pm local time tomorrow, Tuesday."

General O replied, "That sounds fine. Will I then be taken to the **_Taka Maru_**?"

Agent Fong then said, "Yes, we have made arrangements with Captain Saito to be expecting you around 3 pm. A car will be available to us at the airport, and I will drive you to the ship." The agent then looked a little sheepish, had a small grin, and added, "I think the primary reason I was chosen for this mission was that I am oriental and would blend in well to escort you. Once I get you aboard I will then leave the ship. My mission will be finished."

"So at that point I'll pretty much be on my own," said General O. "Do you know when the ship will leave port?"

Admiral Jones replied, "The latest information we have says they plan to cast off at noon tomorrow. That would then put you at Chongjin around 8 am on Friday, December 30th. So you would be there for two days, since the North Koreans told the OKN Line they wanted to depart Chongjin on January 1."

"I see," General O said. "So I will have some free time there."

"Yes," the admiral said, "but we think it would be best if you stayed in your quarters. To get off the ship could be dangerous. Also, you can try to observe exactly what is brought aboard and where it is placed. Our information is that they will be loading five containers. Hopefully, during the trip from Japan to North Korea you will have time to learn all the ship's crew. It will be very important that you're able to distinguish between them and the North Koreans."

The admiral then pulled out a stack of documents and opened up a floor plan for the **Taka Maru** and spread it across the table. He then started to go over it with General O. The rest of the flight to Los Angeles was spent discussing details of the mission. After refueling, the plane was off on the 10 hour flight to Ishigaki. After continuing their discussions for another three hours Admiral Jones said, "General, It's very important that you get well rested. We have a very comfortable bed in the aft compartment. I suggest you go there and try to sleep until we arrive in Japan."

General O said, "Yes, I know that is important. I did not sleep well last night, so even though my internal clock says it's the middle of the day I feel I can sleep. Thanks to each of you for your assistance. And as the Americans say, I'm off to hit the sack."

Chapter 19

Harlan, Kentucky
December 27

Judge Oakes was not in a good mood. He had overeaten on yesterday's Christmas holiday, and he had not slept well last night. He had just sent two men to the pen for robbery. He looked down at his clerk and said, "Okay, call the next case."

The clerk called, "The people versus John Willis Brown."

Several snickers could be heard in the courtroom as John Willis, aka Badass, Brown stood behind the table where Sheriff Sterling sat.

Judge Oakes then looked to the prosecuting attorney's table and said, "Well, what are the charges against Mr. Brown?"

The attorney stood and said, "Attempted kidnapping and murder."

"Call your witnesses," the judge declared.

"Deputy Rosie Cain," the attorney said.

Rosie walked to the front of the court room and was sworn by the bailiff. She then recounted the events that took place on Christmas eve. When she got to the part about Preacher Puss attacking Badass there were giggles throughout the court room. She concluded her testimony.

"Thank you Deputy," said Judge Oakes. "You may be seated."

The judge then looked over at Badass and said, "Mr. Brown, are you not represented by counsel?"

Badass stood and said, "No your honor, I'll represent myself."

"You don't want a court appointed attorney?" asked the judge.

"No your honor. It's a simple case. I'll represent myself," replied Badass

"Suit yourself. Tell us your side," said the judge.

"Well, it was like this, Judge. I was walking past the court house about noon on Christmas eve. I hadn't been feeling well, and I felt kind of faintish. I thought I was going to pass out. I saw the sheriff's car parked in its spot, and noticed it wasn't locked. I figured since it was a public vehicle and all that I could lay down in it for a while until my weak spell passed. So I just jumped in the back seat. I was going to stretch out across the seat but there was a bunch of stuff there, so I decided to lay down on the floorboard. I did, and went to sleep. In a few minutes I woke up, and we were moving. I was on my stomach, and as I started to raise up I felt my hand hit something that felt like metal. I looked, and it was a gun. I don't know how it got there, it wasn't mine. Anyway, I grabbed it in my right hand and started to raise up. I was just getting ready to hand the gun over to the sheriff, who I thought was driving, when that damn pussy cat attacked me. He messed my hand up real good. As it turns out, it was Rosie driving the car. I passed out when that monster cat bit into my arm. The next thing I knew Rosie was hauling me to jail. I didn't do nothing wrong, your honor. I should be suing the sheriff's department for letting that damn cat attack me. I've had to spend all my Christmas holiday in jail. I demand to be released."

Many in the courtroom started laughing. One man slapped his leg and said loudly, "That's the biggest crock I've ever heard."

Judge Oakes slammed down his gavel and said, "Order in this court. Bailiff, if they don't get quiet this second you throw em out."

The judge then looked at Badass and said, "Mr. Brown, I find that story extremely hard to believe."

"It's the gospel truth, your honor," Badass replied.

The judge thought a minute, and then looked at the sheriff and said, "Bert, that story I just heard from Mr. Brown was mighty farfetched. But it could have happened the way he said. There's just not enough evidence to convict. I've got to let him go."

He then looked at Badass and said, "Mr. Brown, you came mighty close to killing Deputy Cain. If it wasn't for Preacher Puss, you'd be standing in front of me charged with murder.

You should go over to the sheriff's department and kiss that cat. I'm going to have to let you go, but I sure wish I didn't. Case dismissed." And he pounded his gavel.

"Thank you judge," replied Badass as he turned and sprinted out of the courtroom.

General Park had spent last night at a motel in Pineville, about 35 miles from Harlan. After leaving Pretty Boy he still hadn't come up with any kind of plan to kill the deserters, so he decided it would be best not to go to Harlan without knowing what to do. He wanted more time to think. After a restless night, he decided he would try and find a way to get all six together, perhaps in a vehicle, and then use a bomb to take them out. But he needed some help. And he couldn't go back to Trigger Green. He just needed someone that knew a little about the deserters, and their habits. Maybe when and where they went for haircuts, or to the grocery store. And he knew that he wanted someone that was pretty stupid.... that wouldn't put together what he was up to. It was then that he remembered seeing a town drunk in Harlan. Maybe he would be the right person. So General Park left Pineville headed for Harlan to try and locate the town drunk.

He knew he could not go back to the Mountain Lair motel for fear of being recognized. He remembered a small bed and breakfast, called The Harlan B&B, and decided that it would likely be safe. He checked in there under the name of

Mr. Park. When he registered he told the clerk that he wasn't sure how long he would be there, but paid a cash deposit of $500, which the clerk readily accepted. After getting settled in his room he headed toward town to look for the drunk.

He drove into town and turned onto Clover Street. He had just passed city hall when he spotted the drunk sitting on a concrete block beside the street. General Park pulled to the curb and sat watching him. He saw a lady walk by and the drunk extend his hand for a handout. She just slapped his hand and continued walking.

General Park got out of his car and walked up to the drunk with a twenty dollar bill in his hand. Bennie immediately spotted the twenty and got a huge smile on his face. He looked at General Park and said, "Hi there friend, you think you could spare that twenty?"

"That and a lot more if you'll agree to help me," General Park replied.

Bennie jumped up, took the twenty, patted the General On the back, and said, "I'm here to help....how can I be of assistance."

General Park said, "My name is Mr. Park. I have a confidential job to do here in Harlan, and I need a little help from someone I can trust. Do you think that might be you?"

"Bennie Sekao's the name, and you can absolutely trust me. My word's my bond!"

General Park replied, "Okay, Mr. Sekao, we can't talk standing here on the street. Let's go sit in my car." The two then walked to the car and got in.

"Let me explain exactly what I need, Mr. Sekao. I work for

the government and am investigating a group of six foreign men that I understand are staying at a farm here in Harlan County. I believe the farm is owned by a pair of brothers..... the Slusher brothers."

Bennie said, "Oh yeah, I know ole Gunsmoke and Booger Slusher. Everyone here knows them. And I've heard about those six guys that are staying there now. I think Sheriff Sterling got them located at the farm after they ran into a little trouble. What did you need to know about them?"

General Park said, "Okay, sounds like you know where the people are that I'm interested in. So let me tell you what I have in mind. First, you must agree to keep everything confidential. You can't say anything about me or what I'm doing here. It's a very hush-hush investigation. I can't even tell you about it, but I can pay you well for cooperating with me. I'll give you one hundred dollars a day for as long as I need to be here. I might finish up in a couple of days, or it might be longer. But each day I'll pay you $100 for assisting me. How does that sound?"

Bennie was drooling by now, and said, "Best offer I've had today. What do we do now?"

General Park reached into his pocket and pulled out a one hundred dollar bill, handed it to Bennie, and said, "Okay, here's what I want you to do. You got to do some background checking for me. I want to know the habits of those six foreigners that are at the Slusher brothers' farm. I want to know where they go and when. Things like when they go get haircuts, when they might go out for a meal.....stuff like that. You think you can inquire around and find out?"

Bennie looked a little puzzled, and said, "Sure. Might take me a little while. But I'll find out for you. When did you need to know?"

"How about if we meet right back here at this same spot at noon tomorrow. If you're here and got that information I'll lay another hundred bill in your hand. Agreed?" the general said.

Bennie said with a big grin, "See you at high noon tomorrow. I'll have all the dope on them guys!" He then got out of the car and started walking. General Park started back to the B&B.

Chapter 20

Ishigaki, Japan
December 27

There was a loud knock on the door. Admiral Jones yelled, "General O, we're approaching Ishigaki Island.... up and at em."

A sleepy response came from behind the door, "Thanks, see you shortly."

General O had slept soundly for almost 7 hours. The aft compartment contained both a bed and shower. The general took a quick shower, shaved, brushed his teeth, did his bathroom duties, dressed, packed his suitcase, stepped through the compartment door and said, "Good morning Admiral Jones and Agent Fong. I know it's probably about 2 pm local time, but it sure seems like morning to me. That was a great rest!"

The admiral and agent were seated at the table. General O joined them. The crew member materialized quickly with orange juice, coffee and buttered toast. Admiral Jones said, "They can stir you up some bacon and eggs if you wish."

General O said, "No, no. This is just perfect. Just something so my stomach won't be empty, and I always have to have this starting fluid. Some call it coffee." He said with a grin.

Agent Fong said, "Our flight went without incident. We're arriving right on time. After we taxi and you finish your snack we'll be off to the *Taka Maru*."

"I've taken quite a few flights, gentlemen, but this was without doubt the best and most memorable," General O said. "Now I just hope and pray that the rest of my mission goes as smoothly."

Ishigaki Island is located south of Japan. It is in the archipelago of the Yaeyama Islands. The city of Ishigaki, with a population of about 48,000, is served by the New Ishigaki Airport, where the Gulfstream G650 had just touched down.

After taxiing to the general aviation terminal the pilot parked the plane. A taxi immediately pulled up near the plane and stopped. The plane's door opened and stairs were extracted to the ground. Before departing General O shook hands with Admiral Jones and said, "I certainly thank you for all your help and assistance. Perhaps we will meet again."

The admiral smiled, shook the general's hand, and said, "I certainly hope so. Best of luck. I feel certain all will go well."

Agent Fong and General O emerged from the plane and descended the stairs. The agent pointed toward the taxi and said, "We thought it best to go to the ship in a cab, so we arranged this ride. The driver is one of our people, so we can still talk freely." The two men jumped into the back seat of the taxi, and they were off.

Captain Ken Saito, master of the ***Taka Maru***, sat at the desk in his quarters going over the crew list. He would have a total crew of 18. In addition to himself there was the chief and second officers, two deck officers, a chief and second engineer, four deck hands, four engine hands, a chief cook, a steward, and the very mysterious engineering officer, Mr. Cho. Captain Saito thought about the phone call he received this morning from Mr. Ito, the CEO of OKN Lines, the company owning the ***Taka Maru***. He had been told that Mr. Cho would arrive sometime today and that he was to personally meet with him upon arrival and show him to his quarters. Mr. Ito told him that Mr. Cho would function as an engineering officer, primarily responsible for the operation of all auxiliary equipment. Further, he was told to have the chief engineer thoroughly acquaint him with all such auxiliary equipment during their passage to North Korea. And finally, Mr. Ito said that he was to extend every courtesy to Mr. Cho and to make absolutely certain that no one else knew of his arrangement. Mr. Ito said simply that Mr. Cho was a very special and important person. The phone call left Captain Saito still guessing who Mr. Cho really worked for and what his mission was. But he knew it wasn't every day he got a phone call from the big man at OKN, so ne figured he'd better comply. He continued his review of the crew members.

———————

The taxi pulled up to the ship's open freight door where fork-lifts were busy loading supplies. Agent Fong looked at General O with a grin and said, "General, your ship awaits you. It has been a great pleasure to get to know you, and I've every confidence that you will be able to complete your mission successfully. I'm sure if you just walk onboard someone will take care of you.'" The two men shook hands and General O opened the door, grabbed his suitcase, and started walking toward the ship.

He had just entered the hull of the vessel when a crew member spotted him and said, "Hey there, you one of our crew?"

General O said, "Yes. My name is Norio Cho. I was told to report to Ken Saito."

The crew person said, "Yes Mr. Cho. Welcome aboard the *Taka Maru*. My name is Fugio Tanaka. I'm the chief engineer, and I understand you will be serving as an engineering officer. I look forward to working with you, and was told when you arrived to take you to the Captain's quarters. Please follow me."

"Enter," Captain Saito replied to the knock on his door.

In walked the chief engineer followed by Mr. Cho. Fugio

Tanaka said, "Captain Saito, this is our new engineering officer, Mr. Norio Cho."

Ken Saito stood from his desk, extended his hand to Mr. Cho, and said, "Welcome to the *Taka Maru*, Mr. Cho. Thank you Fugio."

The chief engineer turned and left the captain's quarters.

"Please....have a seat," the captain said as he again sat at his desk. Mr. Cho sat in a chair in front of the desk.

"Well, Mr. Cho, your arrival has been well announced. Just this morning I had a personal phone call from Mr. Ito, the head of OKN Lines, to tell me that you would be arriving today. He also asked that I take good care of you, and assist in any way possible. He said that you were a very special and important person. And that's about all I know about you. Anything more you could share with me?"

Mr. Cho looked a bit uncomfortable as he said, "Thank you Captain Saito. I am deeply indebted to you and to OKN Lines for your cooperation. The circumstances are such that I am not at liberty to divulge my true purpose, but I can assure you that it does not have anything to do with you, any of your crew, or with OKN Lines. About all I can say is that I'm here on a mission for my government, and your government thought it important enough to ask for OKN Lines' cooperation. I'll certainly try and behave myself and cause you and your crew as few problems as possible."

"I see," the captain replied, "and I understand. The *Taka Maru*, I, and my crew are honored to have you aboard. We will do everything we can to make your stay meaningful and comfortable. You have but to ask. I do have one question. Have you previously served as an engineering officer?"

"I have not," replied Mr. Cho, "but I do have about ten years of naval experience serving aboard a military vessel. I have a technical background, and I think with your help I should be able to discharge the duties of an engineering officer on this cruise."

"I agree," Captain Saito said. "Our chief engineer, Fugio Tanaka, has already been instructed to take you under his wing and show you all the ropes. He's one of my very best. I think you'll enjoy working with him, as well as all the rest of the crew. In just a moment I'll walk you to your quarters. Once you get settled I'll have Fugio walk you around the ship. Tonight at 1800 hours we have a dinner for the entire crew. Everyone will be introduced. We have several new crew members, so your presence will not be obvious. We will pull anchor at noon tomorrow and be off to Chongjin. The trip there will take about 43 hours. So from now until we get to North Korea you will be with Chief Tanaka to learn all your duties. After that, you will be on your own. Is that suitable?"

Mr. Cho extended his hand to Captain Saito and said, "That's perfect, captain. Thanks so much. I look forward to sailing on your ship and to working with you and your crew." The two shook hands vigorously, and then Captain Saito took Mr. Cho to his quarters.

Soon after General O got his clothes unpacked and everything stowed away Fugio Tanaka arrived to take him on a tour of the ship. By the time the tour was finished it was

1800 hours and time for dinner. General O was introduced to the crew as Mr. Norio Cho. The food was good....not great, but good. After dinner General O returned to his quarters, very tired, but excited and encouraged. He got into his pajamas, and then sat on his bunk thinking about his situation. He pulled the beautiful, golden anchor cross from underneath his pajama top and studied it in awe. What beauty, and what a mystery. It felt really good just to be wearing it. And then he looked at his wrist and the special watch. Admiral Jones had told him on the plane trip over that the watch generated a signal that could be picked up anywhere on the ship. He explained that there was a relay box in the same container that held the explosives, and that the relay received the signals from the watch, greatly amplified them, and then transmitted them to those parties that were monitoring. General O knew at least two parties that would be listening; someone in their submarine and someone in Washington, D.C. It was assuring to know that he could be in contact just by speaking and that they would hear anything that he heard. He also realized that if he removed his watch and pressed the recessed cap on its back side three times within 2 seconds the explosives would be detonated and all aboard the **Taka Maru** would be history. He tried not to linger on this thought.

It had been a very good, and long, day. He was tired. He turned out his light and retired.

Chapter 21

Harlan, Kentucky
December 28

Bennie was sitting on the concrete block beside the curb on Clover Street. It was noon. As soon as the car started to approach he recognized it as belonging to Mr. Park. He jumped up and waved, and the car pulled into a parking space parallel to the sidewalk and stopped. Bennie walked to it, opened the passenger door, and got in.

Mr. Park said, "I'm right on time and so are you, Mr. Sekao. Were you able to get the information I wanted?"

Bennie said, "Call me Bennie...everybody does. And I certainly did get it. I got real lucky."

"That's good," Mr. Park replied. "So tell me what you were able to find out."

Bennie said, "Well, after I left you yesterday I walked over to Buckner's Barber Shop. Ole Shorty Buckner runs the place, and I went to grade school with him. Neither one of us finished high school, but Shorty went to barber school and opened up the shop about ten years ago. I spend time there talking to him, the other barbers, and the customers. Lot of people stop in there just to pass the time of day. Course they also have a lot of customers....there to get their hair cut. Anyway, when I walked in there yesterday a guy from the Slusher Farm was there. His name is Ray...don't know his last name. But Ray mostly runs errands for Gunsmoke and Booger, but he stopped by yesterday to get a haircut. How's that for luck?"

"Good," replied Mr. Park. "So what did you find out from this Ray?"

"Well, for a while we just talked about different stuff," Bennie said, "and then I asked him how the Koreans were doing. I told him I hadn't seen them in a while. He said they were fine, and that they'd all be due for their monthly haircuts this Saturday. He said they liked to come into town and get their haircuts and visit that damn cat, called Preacher Puss, at the sheriff's office on the last work day of the month. He said by coming into town then they avoided a lot of the crowd that got out after getting their government checks on the first of the month. So that's just three days from now. That good enough for you? I was afraid to ask about other stuff. Didn't want him to know I was checking them out."

Mr. Park smiled, reached into his pocket and pulled out a one hundred dollar bill and said, "Bennie, that was good work." He handed him the money.

Bennie's eyes got large, and with a big grin he took the

money and said, "Mr. Park, I sure do like doing business with you. What do we do now?"

"What you told me is very interesting. I must think about it, and we'll meet back here tomorrow at noon. By then I hope to have a plan put together, and I may need your help," Mr. Park said.

"Count me in," replied Bennie. "You think about it, and I'll see you here tomorrow." Bennie got out of the car and headed for the bootlegger's. He was thirsty!

———————

"Well, I guess no news is good news," Mayor Fred Knapp said to the sheriff and his deputy as they all enjoyed morning refreshments at Creech Cafe. "But I sure do worry about ole General O. His mission just sounded like it was a very dangerous one....even though they told us nothing about it."

Sheriff Sterling said, "I understand your feelings, Fred. I feel the same way. And we also don't have any idea how long he will be gone. No one knew anything. It could take a few days or even months. Just don't know."

Kyle took a sip of coffee and said, "I think we're all in the same boat. We've grown to really like all those Koreans, and General O is their leader. I do think if something happened to him we would be notified, but that's not much consolation. I guess we just need to watch the news and keep our eyes and ears open. He's only been gone four days, so we just need to try and not think about it."

Fred and Bert nodded in agreement. Fred then said, "Hey guys, I just posted a good one over there on my wall. It'll cheer you up!"

Kyle and Bert stood and walked over to the article Fred had put on his wall. It contained a photograph of a lady holding a baby. The caption below the picture read, 'Baby looks just like mother!'. The article read,

Mr. and Mrs. Robert Watson of Harlan recently took a cruise to the Bahamas. They took their six month old baby son, Robbie, with them. At last Monday's meeting of the Harlan Bridge Club Mrs. Watson told of the following incident that took place on the cruise. She said one day she was pushing baby Robbie in his stroller around the deck, and at least six people stopped her to say how much the baby looked like her. When she got back to their cabin she told her husband what had happened. He seemed a little upset and grabbed the baby, wrapped in a blanket, up in his arms and said he was going for a stroll on the deck. After about twenty minutes he returned to the cabin with a big smile on his face and announced that almost everyone he met told him the baby looked just like him. To that his wife replied, "Well honey, that's because you're holding Robbie upside down!"

Kyle and Bert laughed loudly. Bert said, "I wonder how the rest of that cruise turned out?"

Kyle said, "Hard to say. I think it's time we got back to work."

Trigger Green had walked from his office to the check-out counter behind which Fatso Chapel was sitting reading a book. Trigger said, "Fatso, I just can't shake the thought of what could have happened on Christmas eve at the Slusher Farm. If things had not gone as they did, you and all those other people would have been blown to pieces. How in the world could someone intentionally plan to do something like that? If I ever see that Mr. Chang again I'll make sure his planning days are over."

Fatso replied, "I've had nightmares ever since Christmas eve about it. And that Wong Chang guy seemed like a nice man. A little strange, perhaps, but a nice man."

"You just can't tell a book from its cover," replied Trigger.

"Hey Trigger, you know why elephants have wrinkles?"

Trigger just looked at Fatso.

Fatso said with a chuckle, "Because they're so hard to iron."

Trigger threw up his arms and started walking back to his office.

Chapter 22

Chongjin, North Korea
December 29

The huge doors to their warehouse were open, and jumbo fork-lifts were in the process of moving the five containers out onto the pier. From there large overhead cranes would lift them onto the ***Taka Maru*** after it arrived tomorrow morning around 7 am. Admiral Sung had been advised that the ship had left Ishigaki on schedule yesterday at noon.

"Careful, careful," the admiral shouted to the fork-lift operator moving the container with the red letters 'USE EXTREME CAUTION'. The other four had previously been moved. This one, containing the nuclear warhead, was the one he was most concerned about. "Make certain you don't hit anything or drop it," he shouted. The operator nodded, but had a disgruntled look on his face. He moved the load slowly into place on the pier.

Commander Shin said, "Good, good. That got them all out, Admiral. How do you want them guarded?"

"We've got ten men, so station 3 out here on guard for 4 hours shifts. Let the Chief Petty Officer stay in the warehouse with us. I don't think we'll have any trouble, but as important as this mission is for the Supreme Leader we sure don't want any problem," replied Admiral Sung.

"Will do," Commander Shin said.

East China Sea

The ***Taka Maru*** was plowing at about 25 knots through the northern tip of the East China Sea and was just entering the southernmost section of the Sea of Japan. Japan was off their starboard, and South Korea off their port.

Captain Saito and second officer Kozo Yamazaki were on the bridge. The captain said, "Kozo, what's your latest estimate on our arrival at Chongjin?"

The second officer replied, "We've had very favorable conditions so far. It looks like we'll likely dock at about 0600 tomorrow morning. About an hour ahead of schedule."

"No problem with that," the captain replied.

There was a knock on the door. Captain Saito turned and opened it. Mr. Cho and chief engineer Fugio Tanaka stood on the other side. Fugio said, "Captain, we have worked our way midship and I thought this might be a good time to show Mr. Cho the bridge. Is it convenient?"

"Certainly," replied Captain Saito. "Come right in."

The captain looked at Mr. Cho and said, "So is Fugio giving you the grand tour?"

"Indeed," Mr. Cho replied. "You have a very interesting ship. Most of the equipment I'm familiar with, and Chief Tanaka has explained in great detail the function and operation of all that were new to me. Everything is going quite well. I did notice a large empty space on the foredeck. Is that where the North Korean containers are to be placed?"

"Yes," replied Captain Saito. "There will be only five of them, and they requested that they be placed where they could be easily accessed. I don't know what kind of equipment they have, but they're bringing a team of 12 people to work on it and to then assemble it when we get to Venezuela. Must be important stuff."

Chief Tanaka then gave Mr. Cho a tour of the bridge, explaining the function of all the equipment and instruments. At the conclusion Mr. Cho said, "Most impressive. Are we running on schedule?"

Kozo replied, "Actually we're running a bit ahead. Should make port by 0600."

Mr. Cho and Chief Tanaka then turned to leave the bridge. The chief said, "Many thanks, see you guys later."

The two then continued their tour of the ship.

Pyongyang, North Korea

Deputy Pak Pong-hae and Lieutenant Hwang Pyong-ju stood before the desk of Supreme Leader Kim Jong-un. Kim was completing a mid-afternoon snack. He had just eaten 3 cheeseburgers and 2 orders of fries. He belched, and said, "Deputy Pak, do I understand correctly that Lieutenant Hwang has been caught relaying state information?"

Deputy Pak replied, "Yes Supreme Leader, that is correct. He was caught in the act of using the internet to send highly classified information to a foreign power."

Kim looked intently at Hwang and said, "And who was the foreign power?"

Pak replied, "The United States."

Sweat had formed on the brow of Lieutenant Hwang. He closed his eyes.

Kim reached in his desk, pulled out his revolver, and shot the Lieutenant directly between the eyes. He stumbled backward, and fell to the floor.

Kim hit the intercom button and said, "Get in here and get this traitor out of my office."

Two military men rushed into Kim's office. One was carrying a mop and bucket, the other a can of disinfectant and paper towels. They rolled the dead man over, mopped up the blood from the floor, sprayed it with the disinfectant, and wiped it clean. They then placed the paper towels and disinfectant in the bucket, and with it and the mop in one hand the two lifted the deceased by his arms and dragged him out of the supreme leader's office. The total time was only 55 seconds. Had they taken longer than one minute Kim would have shot them. He demanded efficiency.

Kim then stared at Deputy Pak, who was also beginning to sweat. Kim said, "What information exactly did the traitor pass to the U.S.?"

Deputy Pak said, "We are uncertain how much, but we know it involved the nuclear attack. He was stationed with the 12 chosen for the mission. As best we can tell, he alerted the U.S. about the planned attack."

Kim then pointed the revolver at his deputy and pulled the trigger, shooting him directly in the heart. He slumped to the floor. Kim again punched the intercom. "Got another one."

The two man team rushed in, repeated the clean up, and were gone in 50 seconds. Kim looked at his watch and nodded.

Kim got a worried look on his fat face. He sat back in his chair and thought, *So the enemy knows my plan. That could be a problem, but perhaps not. I'll alert Admiral Sung to be extra cautious and proceed. I'll tell him that if any enemy tries to stop the ship he should immediately take steps to destroy it. My plan will either work, or, worst case, it will fail but no one will find any evidence of the attempt.*

Kim punched the intercom and said, "I want two milkshakes, one vanilla and one chocolate."

Sea of Japan

It was evening. General O, aka Mr. Cho, lay on his bunk. It had been a good and full day. He had accomplished everything planned for the day. Chief Tanaka had shown him all the auxiliary equipment and fully explained to him how each piece worked and its overall function. But he knew that the dangerous portion of his mission would start tomorrow. He had confidence that he could perform his duties without any of the North Koreans suspecting him. He did have concerns that one or more might possibly recognize him, but he doubted that. When he was with the North Korean military his hair was cut very short. He had now let his hair grow long. Also, he had gained about twenty pounds. Previously he wore glasses, but now he had contacts. Certainly the odds were in his favor....but still he worried. He then felt the golden anchor cross pressing against his stomach. It felt very comforting. He could do this.

Chapter 23

Harlan, Kentucky
December 29

It was noon. Bennie jumped up from the concrete block he was sitting on, opened the car door, got in, and said, "Right on time, Mr. Park. Did you figure out what we're going to do?"

General Park looked at Bennie and said, "Yes, I've been giving it a great deal of thought, and I have a plan for us."

"Lay it on me," responded Bennie.

"It goes like this," General Park replied. "Saturday is the last business day of the month, so you said that would be the day the Koreans come in town for their haircuts."

"Yes," said Bennie. "And to visit with that damn cat at the sheriff's office."

"Well, forget that," General Park replied. "I'm interested in their visit to the barber shop. What I want you to do is the following. After Ray has parked their van and they've all gone into the shop, I want you to stagger by, playing like you've had a little too much to drink."

Bennie interrupted, "Oh, I'm good at that. No problem at all."

General Park continued, "So you stagger by the van and you pretend to fall beside it. When you do you stick a box up under the van's fender. It's magnetic, so It'll stick there easily. You think you could do that without anyone seeing you?"

"Piece of cake," Bennie replied. "But what will be in the little box?"

"It's just a tracking device, and I'll be able to hear what they're talking about," General Park lied.

"Well, that couldn't hurt anything. Yeah, I can do that. Do I get my reward?"

General Park pulled out another one hundred dollar bill and handed it to Bennie. "And on Saturday, I'll have another one waiting for you after you've attached the box."

"Mr. Park, you're really a great guy to work with," Bennie said as he took the money with a smile."

Mr. Park replied, "The only problem we have is we don't know exactly when they will arrive for their haircuts."

Bennie said, "They always come early, so it'll likely be sometime just after the shop opens at 8 am."

General Park replied, "Okay, so let's meet right here at 7:30 on Saturday morning. Then we'll drive to the barber shop and park where we can watch for the van to arrive. Then, we'll wait a few minutes for them to get all set in the shop and you can then do your thing. After you've attached the box you'll come back to my car for your reward. That sound okay?"

"Perfect," replied Bennie. See you Saturday morning at 7:30." He then got out of General Park's car and began walking to get refreshment.

General Park thought, *I sure picked the right guy for this job. Dumb as a rock. I've now got to get the bomb put together and into a suitable box. Good thing I remembered to get more explosives from Pretty Boy Maggard before I left Knoxville. I'm sure I can get all the other needed parts without a problem. So if all goes as planned I'll be back in Knoxville Saturday afternoon and ready to fly home.*

———————

Mayor Knapp was posting a new article on the back wall in Creech Cafe when Sheriff Sterling and Deputy Potter walked in. Fred waved to them and said, "You boys have a seat, I'll be there with the coffee in just a second."

Kyle replied, "No rush Fred, take your time and make sure you get that new article up properly." He grinned, looked at Bert and added, "I'll be interested to hear about it."

After a few minutes Fred arrived at the table where his two friends were seated. He said, "Good afternoon, guys. That was a real good one I just put up. Can I make your day by telling you all about it?"

Bert said, "Fred, we do enjoy your coffee, but what we really enjoy most is listening to your stories. We're all ears!"

"Well....twist my arm," Fred replied. "Okay, here's the story. You know Mac Johnson, the **Harlan Daily Enterprise** reporter. As you know, Mac is a member of Pastor Raymond Bell's New Hope Baptist Church, and occasionally reports some of Raymond's better stories in the **Enterprise's** *Tickle Bone* column. The posting I just made was one of those. Mac reported three stories Pastor Bell recently told, as follows":

#1. A little girl was watching her mother put cold cream on her face before bedtime. The little girl said, "Mother, why do you put that stuff on your face?" Her mother replied, "To make me beautiful." The next morning the little girl saw her mother removing the cold cream from her face. The little girl asked, "Did you give up?"

#2. A little boy asked his father, "Daddy, how big is the world?". The father replied, "Don't know son." The next day he asked his father, "Daddy, how old is the moon?. The father said, "Don't know son." The following day he asked, "Daddy, how much water is in the oceans?" His father said, "Don't know son." The little boy then said to his father, "Daddy, do you mind me asking you questions? The father said, "Of course not son. How would you ever learn anything if you didn't ask questions?"

#3. The 16 year old son of a pastor was chatting with a lady in the congregation. The boy said, "When I was younger I had a bad drug problem." The lady was astounded. Her mouth dropped open and her eyes widened, and she said, "I cannot believe that.

You, the son of our pastor, had a drug problem? The boy responded, "Yeah, every Sunday morning my parents drugged me to Sunday School. Then they drugged me to church. On Wednesday nights they drugged me to prayer meeting. I had a real drug problem!"

"Raymond does come up with some good ones," Bert said with a smile. "I'm glad Mac was there to report them.... they are cute."

Kyle laughed and said, "Laughter is good for the soul."

Fred asked, "Still no word at all from General O?"

"Nothing....quiet as can be," Bert replied. "I suspect we won't hear anything more until the mission is over. And, of course, we don't have any idea how long that will be. It's just a waiting game."

"He remains in our prayers," Fred replied.

Bert then stood and said, "Okay Kyle, let's head over to Maggard's Grocery. I have something I want to ask Fatso and Trigger."

Fred replied, "Anything I should know?"

Bert said, "No, it's just a rumor. A couple of folks have told me they saw a person driving a car in Harlan that looked a lot like that Wong Park fellow. I thought I'd ask at Maggard's if they knew anything about it. Since he almost killed us all, including Fatso, I figured they'd tell me if they knew anything."

"Good luck, Bert," the Mayor replied, "it sure would be good to capture that nut."

When he heard the front door open Fatso looked up from the book he was reading to see Sheriff Sterling and Deputy Potter. "Well, well, well. Harlan County's finest. Good to see you boys."

Bert replied, "Hey Fatso, how you doing? We had a question for you and Trigger, you mind asking him to join us?"

"Sure thing sheriff," Fatso replied. "But first, you have to tell me what you do with a green elephant?"

Kyle said with a big smile, "You wait till he ripens."

"You guys are getting smarter," Fatso said as he punched the intercom button. "Hey Trigger, the law's out here and wants you to come join us."

"Be right out," Trigger was heard to say, and in a moment joined the other three.

Trigger shook hands with Bert and Kyle and said, "How can we be of service?"

Bert responded, "I've had two different people tell me that they saw someone driving around Harlan that looked a lot like Wong Park. Either of you heard anything?"

Trigger looked at Fatso, who shook his head negatively, and said, "No, not a word. But I'll tell you one thing. If I do run into him I'll change the looks of his face so that no one else will ever recognize him. I'd just love to have five minutes with that bastard. He just about killed us all."

"I thought that would be your response, Trigger," Bert

replied. "But I needed to ask. Please do me the favor of a phone call if you hear anything....taking care of Mr. Park is our business. Don't want to see you get in trouble."

Trigger nodded affirmatively, as did Fatso, who then asked, "Hey boys, you know what's gray and lights up?"

Bert and Kyle turned and started for the door.

"An electric elephant," shouted Fatso with a chuckle.

Chapter 24

Chongjin, North Korea
December 30

It was 6 am, dark and foggy. Admiral Sung and Commander Shin stood on the pier beside their five containers looking for the ***Taka Maru***. The ship was due.

The admiral said, "Commander, it's going to be a busy day. First we have to carefully get the containers loaded, and then we must meet with the ship's crew. Our supreme leader told me last night that a spy had been discovered in our ranks, and there is every reason to believe that the U.S. is aware of our planned attack. If that's the case, then one or more of the ship's crew could be bogus. I told our leader that after we got the cargo loaded we would demand a meeting of all the ship's crew. I'll tell the captain that we just want to have a 'get-acquainted' meeting, but the real purpose will be to carefully evaluate each member to see if any seem suspicious."

Shin replied, "Yes, that would be wise. Who was the spy that was uncovered?"

Sung said, "His name was Lieutenant Hwang Pyong-ju. He was stationed with us during a part of our training. Deputy Pak Pong-hae discovered him, and the two informed our supreme leader. Neither of them are still among the living."

The commander replied, "I remember Hwang. He seemed a good soldier. Too bad he was rotten."

The two looked intently into the fog, in the direction the ship would be coming. Occasional fog horns could be heard.... otherwise, it was totally quiet. Light from high intensity lamps located at the top of poles along the pier bounced off moisture from dew on the containers and pier decking.

Suddenly a loud horn blasted through the fog. The two stared in its direction. Very, very slowly the shape of a ship's bow materialized. "That's her," said Admiral Sung. "Round up the rest of our gang....they might be of some help in getting the ship tied up."

"Yes sir," Commander Shin replied as he turned and started to run toward the warehouse where the other soldiers were quartered.

The admiral watched in awe as the giant ship inched closer to the pier. Three port employees took their stations along the pier, ready to grab the docking lines when they were tossed from the **Taka Maru**. Ever so slowly the ship maneuvered into its slip. Side thrusters started to push the vessel toward the dock. Ship's crew could be seen standing on the bow, amidship, and on the stern with docking lines at the ready.

Commander Shin and the other eight soldiers came trotting up beside Admiral Sung. Shin said, "Looks like everything is well under control, admiral."

"It does," Sung said. "The captain seems extra cautious in his docking maneuvers....and he should be with this fog."

Just then all three ship crew tossed their docking lines to the port employees. Each grabbed a line and secured it. The *Taka Maru* was docked.

A huge loading ramp on the ship's side located amidship was then released and allowed to fall onto the dock. It was hinged at the bottom, and came to rest nearly horizontal on the pier. After a couple of minutes two of the ship's crew walked across it.

Admiral Sung approached the two. He smiled, offered his hand, and said, "Gentlemen, my name is Admiral Sung Ho-jun. I'm in charge of the cargo and personnel you are loading here."

Lt. Commander Shin walked up beside Sung, who then added, "And this is Lt. Commander Shin In-Tak, my second in command. We are all members of the North Korean military."

Captain Saito shook hands with the two and said, "Greetings. I'm Ken Saito, master of the *Taka Maru*. This gentleman is Chief Hiroto Hotaka, my chief officer."

Captain Saito then looked at the containers resting on the pier and said, "I assume those are the containers that we are to load."

Admiral Sung replied, "They are. But you are not to start loading until this fog lifts, and until I give the okay. The cargo is very delicate, and I want my personnel to be involved in watching the loading and directing the positioning on deck."

Captain Saito eyed Admiral Sung for a moment, and then said, "As you wish. I would suggest you and your personnel come aboard and get settled in your quarters, and then we can begin loading the containers when you give the okay."

Sung and Shin nodded in agreement, and the twelve soldiers followed Captain Saito and Chief Hotaka aboard the ship.

After the soldiers were shown their quarters they returned to the warehouse, retrieved their gear, and got settled aboard. After about an hour Captain Saito knocked on the cabin door of Admiral Sung.

"Yes, come in," the admiral shouted.

Captain Saito entered and said, "If you and your crew are ready we could begin loading the containers."

"Yes," Admiral Sung said, "I'll pass the word to my people and we'll all be back up on deck in about 15 minutes to assist with the loading. After that, I would like to have a little get-acquainted session, if that is agreeable. Perhaps all your crew and mine could meet anywhere that would be suitable and we could introduce ourselves. I thought this would be helpful since we're all going to be onboard together for the next couple of weeks."

Captain Saito replied, "Certainly. Could we possibly do it this evening when we have dinner? If so, we could all meet in the galley."

"I think that would be fine," said Admiral Sung. "1800 hours?"

"1800 hours will work. In the meantime I'll see your crew on deck in about 15 minutes to begin loading the containers."

Mr. Cho had previously had a discussion with Captain Saito about how he wanted to be involved in loading the North Korean's cargo. The captain had agreed to allow him to work on the deck directing the crane operator in positioning the containers. Captain Saito walked directly to Mr. Cho's cabin and shared with him the conversation he just had with Mr. Sung. Mr. Cho and the captain then walked together onto deck. The crane was operated by Fugio Tanaka, the chief engineer. Chief Tanaka was already in the cab of the crane ready to load the containers. Four of the North Koreans had left the ship and were standing on the pier beside their cargo to assist in securing the crane's hooks to the containers. The other eight, including the admiral and commander, were on the deck in the approximate position where they wanted the containers positioned. Captain Saito introduced Mr. Cho, Chief Tanaka, and three other of his deck crew to the admiral and commander. After a discussion about where the cargo should be placed the transfer began. All went very smoothly until the very last container was ready for loading. Mr. Cho noticed that it was marked with bright red letters requesting caution. He could tell that all the North Koreans seemed highly excited about its movement, and thought it had to contain the nuclear warhead. Admiral Sung shouted loudly at Chief Tanaka as the last container was moved on deck. He admonished the chief to take it very slowly and carefully. Finally it was positioned, and all seemed highly relieved.

Admiral Sung then turned to Captain Saito and said, "I'm pleased to have that job completed. We will see you and your crew in the galley at 1800 hours."

The ship's crew all nodded in agreement, and then all went their separate ways. Mr. Cho knew the dinner could prove difficult for him, but at least he had already met the North Koreans and so far so good. He returned to his quarters to think about how the cargo was positioned on deck and the upcoming dinner meeting.

Captain Saito stood at the head of the line in the galley personally welcoming each of the North Korean soldiers. All twelve arrived at one time, with Admiral Sung and Commander Shin leading the other ten. The crew of the **Taka Maru** had already passed through the galley and after receiving their food were seated in the adjacent mess deck. The soldiers took a seat at a long table that had been put in place just for them, making the room a bit crowded. After all had finished their meal Captain Saito stood in the middle of the room and said, "Gentlemen, I would like to personally welcome everyone to the **Taka Maru**. I think I've met each of you, and now I would like to introduce each of my crew." He then walked over to the table where his crew was seated and introduced each, asking that they stand and give their name, title, and a brief history of their maritime experience.

When Captain Saito pointed to Mr. Cho he stood and said, "My name is Norio Cho, engineering officer. I just joined the crew of the *Taka Maru* in Ishigaki. Prior to that I had served for eight years as engineering officer aboard the cruise ship *MS Asuka II*, owned by Nippon Yusen Kaisha. I took the position on board the *Asuka II* after retiring from the Japan Maritime Self-Defense Force (JMSDF) with the rank of Lt. Commander. I left the *Asuka II* in order to get away from the damn tourists. After eight years I just couldn't take any more of them." Laughter broke out among the soldiers and *Taka Maru* crew. Mr. Cho then took his seat, and Captain Saito continued introducing the rest of his crew.

After the ship's crew were all introduced, Admiral Sung stood and introduced himself and then each of his soldiers. After the introductions he said, "I thank Captain Saito for this meeting. I felt it important that we all know each other since we'll be together aboard the *Taka Maru* for at least the next week. We look forward to the trip."

The admiral had previously met with all his soldiers and had told them to carefully observe each of the ship's crew to see if anything looked suspicious. He had instructed them to mingle with the crew after the meal and introductions to see if any seemed bogus. The admiral headed straight to Mr. Cho and said, "Your background was very interesting. Are you aware of the prior history of the *Asuka II*?"

Mr. Cho replied, "Somewhat. I know that she was originally built by the Mitsubishi Heavy Industries shipyard in Nagasaki as **Crystal Harmony** for Crystal Cruises."

The admiral nodded in agreement, and then asked, "How long did you serve in JMSDF?"

"Twenty years," responded Mr. Cho. "I retired at first opportunity. I loved duty aboard ship and my future at JMSDF was beginning to look like getting stuck ashore."

"I see," replied the admiral. He turned and began questioning other members of the ship's crew.

Mr. Cho began positioning himself to exit the mess deck. One of the soldiers stopped him and asked, "You look familiar. Have you spent time in North Korea?"

"No, today was my first North Korean port to visit," replied Mr. Cho.

"Must have been someone else," replied the soldier.

Mr. Cho continued moving off the mess deck, and after a few minutes arrived back in his quarters. He felt very relieved. He felt that the brief conversations with the admiral and the soldier went well, and that neither either recognized him or suspected he was not really a crew member. He retired and slept well.

Lt. Commander Shin walked with the admiral back to their quarters. Shin asked, "So, what do you think? Did you observe anyone suspicious?"

Admiral Sung said, "Nothing definite. I asked that Mr. Cho a couple of questions that he answered correctly, but I had a feeling about him. And then one of our men said he thought Cho looked familiar, but couldn't quite place him. Nothing for sure, but I think we should keep an eye on him."

Lt. Commander Shin nodded agreement, and the two returned to their quarters.

Chapter 25

Harlan, Kentucky
December 31

General Park sat in his room at the Harlan Bed & Breakfast. It was early Saturday morning. He would have a light breakfast at about 6:45 am, and then drive into town and meet with Bennie at 7:30 am. His suitcase was all packed. If everything went as planned he would not be returning to the B&B, but would drive to Knoxville immediately after concluding his business and would then be back home in Pyongyang no later than Monday. He looked at the bomb resting on his bed. He knew it contained enough explosives to easily demolish the minivan and all six of the defectors. He had constructed the bomb inside a box that would be held in place by a strong magnet. It would be Bennie's job to attach it to the fender of the minivan. He would then detonate the bomb using the remote device he carried in his coat pocket.

He thought about the consequences of his actions. At least seven people would be killed, the six deserters and the van driver, and perhaps more if others were close by when the explosion occurred. The deserters deserved it, but he did feel badly for the driver and any other completely innocent people that might die. After the bomb was in place and the van left the barber shop he would follow it until it got to a location where there were no others around and then detonate it. That way the driver would be the only innocent victim. He then thought about how nice the people were here in Harlan. Those here at the B&B had treated him like family. He was not accustomed to such warmth and hospitality. But he had a job to do. He grabbed the bomb from off the bed and placed it in a small canvas bag beside his suitcase. After breakfast he would load them in his car and be off.

The clock in General Park's car read 7:25 am. He saw Bennie sitting on the concrete block waiting for him. He pulled to the curb and Bennie jumped in. "How you doing this fine morning Mr. Park?"

General Park replied, "Good, good. Glad to see you're right on time. We just need to drive and park where we can observe the Slusher Brothers' minivan when it arrives. You direct me to the best place."

"I can do that," Bennie replied. He told General Park to make several turns and then found a parking space just about a block east of the barber shop, which was next door to Creech Cafe and directly across the street from the Harlan County Court House. The clock in the car now indicated it was 7:40 am.

"Hey, there they are. They're really early today, the barber shop doesn't even open until 8 am," said Bennie as he and General Park watched the minivan park directly in front of the barber shop.

The two watched as the doors to the minivan opened and people started to get out. They then started to walk across the street toward the court house.

"Looks like they're going to visit that damn cat in the sheriff's department," Bennie said.

"Why would they do that?" asked General Park.

"Beats me," Bennie replied. "They just like that cat for some reason. They wouldn't like her if she did to them what she done to me. Damn thing'll eat you up."

All those from the van walked together as a group and entered the door to the sheriff's department.

General Park said, "Well, at least it gives us a good chance to go ahead and get the listening device planted on their van." He reached inside the canvas bag, pulled out the bomb, and said, "Here it is Bennie. All you have to do is stagger up the street, playing like you've had one too many, and when you get beside the van you act like you stumble. When you're down beside the front fender on their van just reach up under the fender and slap this device in place. The magnet will hold it. You think you can do it?"

"Piece of cake," Bennie replied. "And then I come back here and you'll give me my reward, right?"

"Right," the general said as Bennie grabbed the bomb, opened the door, and started staggering down the street.

Deputy Rosie Cain looked up from the counter behind

which she worked and said, "Well, well. I do believe it's the Preacher Puss fan club. You boys are out early today."

"Early bird gets the worm," Ray said. "Yeah, the guys are in town for their monthly haircuts and wanted to come a little early to have a visit with their favorite cat before getting their ears lowered. I hope you don't mind."

"No, no. Not at all. And I'm sure they have made Preacher Puss's day," replied Rosie.

Preacher Puss had observed her friends entering, and had jumped up from her ledge and pounced onto the desk located directly below. All the visitors had lined up to take turns petting her. She responded with a constant series of very loud purrs, arched back, and vigorous tail swishing, and would occasionally roll over to allow her tummy to be tickled. It looked almost like she had a big smile on her face.

Ray then said, "Rosie, we brought some treats and play-things for her. Do you think it would be okay if we took her out in the court house lawn for a little exercise?"

"Oh, I'm sure she would enjoy that. She needs to get out of the office. You go right ahead," Rosie replied.

Ray grabbed Preacher Puss and all headed back out the door to the court house lawn. Once there, Ray gently placed the cat on the ground and reached into his pocket for the package of Whisker-Lickin treats. He opened it and gave her one. She gobbled it down and looked expectantly for another. The five others then formed a large circle around Preacher Puss and started to roll a tennis ball toward her. She ran to it and kicked it with her front paws. It rolled across the circle to another of the Koreans, who then rolled it back toward her.

They kept up this game of ball with Preacher Puss for another 15 minutes, with occasional breaks to give her one or two more Whisker-Lickin treats.

General Park had been watching from his car. Bennie had successfully placed the bomb on the Slusher Brothers' van, had returned and gotten his $100 reward. The two of them sat watching the men playing with Preacher Puss on the court house lawn. The general thought how contented they all seemed to be. He imagined getting satisfaction from playing with a cat. After a few minutes he saw the one gather the cat and they all went back in the sheriff's department. General Park said to Bennie, "Well, it looks like the playtime is over. It's just past 8 am so I guess they are ready for their haircuts."

"Looks that way," Bennie replied.

Ray then came back out of the sheriff's department followed by the Koreans. As they paraded across the court house lawn headed for the barber shop it suddenly struck General Park. He said, "Bennie, there should be six of the Koreans....but I only count five plus that fellow they call Ray. Where's the sixth Korean?"

"Damn if I know," replied Bennie.

General Park said,"Well, I have to know. I need all six of them for my mission. How about you go down and go in the barber shop after they go in and do the chit-chat for a while and then ask about the sixth one. You can think of some way to ask without raising suspision."

"Is that worth another hundred?" Bennie asked.

"It is," said the general.

Bennie jumped out of the car and headed for the barber shop. After about a half hour he returned to the car, got in, and said, "I found out about #6. They said he was out of the country on some kind of mission and had no idea when he would return. How about my hundred?"

The general thought about this for about a minute, and then said, "Yes, yes, I have it right here. And I'm going to give you an extra hundred as a bonus. This concludes our business." General Park then reached into his pocket and peeled off two one hundred dollar bills and handed them to Bennie. He then patted him on the back, shook his hand, and said, "Thanks for all your help. Perhaps our paths will cross again."

With eyes large as saucers Bennie replied, "Yeah boy, I sure hope so. It's really been a pleasure working with you Mr. Park. You look me up any old time you need something done and I'll be delighted to help." Bennie opened the car door, got out, and headed for refreshments.

General Park had made a decision. He knew that the missing Korean was General O, and that he could not return home without telling the supreme leader that General O had been eliminated along with the other five deserters. So it made no sense to kill the five. He would not be returning to North Korea.

He grabbed the canvas bag, got out of his car, and started walking toward the minivan. When he got beside it he reached up under the fender and extracted the bomb. He placed it in the canvas bag along with its remote detonator. He then started walking across the street toward the sheriff's department.

"Yes sir, could I help you?" Rosie asked the stranger standing just inside the doorway.

General Park replied, "Yes you may. I would like to see the sheriff."

"Please have a seat and I'll check with Sheriff Sterling," Rosie replied.

"Thank you," General Park said as he pulled up the desk chair and seated himself. Rosie turned and walked into the sheriff's office. It was then that General Park remembered he was carrying a pistol. He reached under his coat and removed the gun. Preacher Puss had been watching the stranger intently from her ledge above the front door. When she saw him extract the pistol she began her jump with claws extended. But then she saw him lay the pistol on the desk, and she pulled in her claws just as she landed atop his head. General Park reached up and removed the cat to his lap. He began gently stroking her. Preacher Puss responded with a loud purr and rapid tail swishing.

"I see you've met Preacher Puss," Sheriff Sterling said as he entered the reception room.

General Park looked up at the sheriff and said, "Is that her name? Preacher Puss? That's a strange name for a cat."

"That's a strange cat," Bert replied. "How can I help you?"

General Park slowly handed the cat to the sheriff and said, "I think we need to talk."

Bert placed Preacher Puss back on her bed atop the ledge and said, "Sure, come on into my office. Leave the pistol on the desk, my deputy will take care of it."

"Of course," said the general as he grabbed his canvas bag and followed Sheriff Sterling into his office.

General Park then told Bert the entire story about his mission to kill the six North Korean deserters. He explained that he was a general in the North Korean army and had been sent on the mission by supreme leader Kim Jong-un. He explained how his first attempt on Christmas eve had failed, and then about his return to try a second time, but when he learned of General O's absence he decided that he could not possibly fulfill his mission. He then said, "So Mr. Sheriff, I am placing myself in your custody and am hereby requesting political asylum."

Bert nodded, smiled, stood, walked over to General Park and extended his hand. The two shook hands. Bert then pressed the intercom button on his desk and spoke to Rosie, "Please get one of the Slusher brothers on the phone for me."

Chapter 26

Chongjin, North Korea
January 1

Fortunately, there was no fog this morning. The ***Taka Maru*** cast off at 9 am, and the port city of Chongjin could now be seen over her stern. The trip was underway.

Admiral Sung sat in his quarters after having been on the bridge to observe the ship's departure. He knew that the critical time for him and his men was rapidly approaching. He would allow the ship to get through the Sea of Japan and into the North Pacific before taking command. That would happen sometime tomorrow. Yesterday he had found a space between containers in the belly of the ship that he requested from Capt. Saito be reserved for his use where he could meet with his men and conduct official business. He had told the captain that this space was strictly off limits for any of the ship's crew. Captain Saito agreed, and the two of them referred to the space as the 'belly room'. Later yesterday the admiral gathered all his soldiers in the belly room and went over their plans for commandeering the ship.

Sea of Japan

Captain Saito and Norio Cho were seated at the navigation table in the bridge. Second officer Kozo Yamazaki was standing at the helm guiding the giant ship out into the Sea of Japan.

The captain said, "Mr. Cho, perhaps this is none of my business, but that North Korean bunch gives me the willies. There's something about them that just doesn't ring true. I suspect you might have some idea what that is, but I respect your need to keep the information confidential."

Mr. Cho replied, "I understand what you say, and I agree with you. If there was anything I could tell you that would help, I would. But the truth is, I do know a few things about them that you do not, but sharing any of those things would not assist you at this time. I think we just have to let things play out and make any necessary adjustments on the fly."

Captain Saito thought for a moment and then said, "I just get the feeling that the cargo we took on in Chongjin is of very special significance. As master of this ship I am very concerned that my ship and her crew are not placed in jeopardy."

"That I understand," said Mr. Cho. "Please believe me when I say that I have that same desire. If at anytime I feel the ship or her crew are in danger I'll report the circumstances to you immediately."

"Thank you Mr. Cho, I do feel you would," replied Captain Saito.

––––––

Harlan, Kentucky

"Good morning Gunsmoke and Booger," Rosie said. "You two are looking well." The brothers had just walked into the sheriff's department.

Gunsmoke said, "Good morning to you, Rosie. Always good to see your cheerful face." He then turned around and looked up above the door to the ledge where Preacher Puss sat looking with great interest at the Slusher Brothers. Gunsmoke reached up and stroked the cat several times and said, "Ole girl, are you keeping the peace?". Preacher Puss responded by purring loudly. Booger then reached up and gave her several pats and pets, and then she jumped to the floor and started rubbing against the brothers' ankles.

"She sure remembers you two," Rosie said. "That cat has a remarkable brain."

"Yeah, we thought the world of her for the short time she lived with us. She's just a very special animal."

"She is," Rosie responded. "I think Bert is waiting for you two, why don't you go right on in."

"Thanks," the brothers said in unison as they walked toward the sheriff's office.

Bert stood as soon as he saw the brothers enter his office. He walked around his desk and shook hands with them. He then asked if they would have a seat, and said, "Boys, I really appreciate so much your coming over this morning. As I told you on the phone, I have a very special situation, and I hope that you might be able to help me with it. If you would excuse me for just a moment I'll go get someone I want you to meet."

Bert then turned and walked out the back of his office and down the hall to his holding facility. He said, "General Park, if you would join me I have a couple of people I'd like you to meet." The general said, "Certainly Mr. Sheriff." The two walked back to Bert's office.

The brothers stood when the two entered. Bert said, "Gentlemen, this is General Park Chang-Sun of the North Korean army."

The brothers each shook hands with the general and told him their names. All then took a seat.

Bert said, "Let me start by saying that General Park has voluntarily turned himself in to me and desires to apply for political asylum. He was sent here by the North Korean dictator Kim Jung-un on a mission to kill the six North Koreans staying at your farm. He is the person that put together the bomb disguised as a Christmas gift that almost killed us all on Christmas eve. He then made a second attempt yesterday when Ray brought the North Koreans in for their monthly haircuts. Fortunately, he aborted that attempt when he discovered that General O was not in the group. He realized that he could not return to North Korea having failed in his mission, so he turned himself in to me and has fully cooperated. As I said, he desires to apply for political asylum. In my judgment it will likely be granted, but will take a few months for the paperwork to be processed and evaluated. In the meantime, rather than hold him in jail I was wondering if you would consider letting him join his fellow countrymen at your farm. He could work for you just as do the other six. I know I'm asking a lot from you, but the only other choice I have is to hold him in custody. If you don't think it would work, I certainly understand."

Gunsmoke looked at Booger. Slowly, Booger started nodding affirmatively. Gunsmoke then said, "You're in luck, General Park, we just happen to have a vacancy!" He walked over to the general and patted him on his back and said, "General O's room is available. We don't know for how long, but you're welcome to occupy it until he returns, and then we'll find other accommodations for you. Welcome to the United States!"

General Park's eyes seemed to moist as he said, "I really don't know what to say....other than a very sincere 'thank you'. I will do my very best to try and make up to you for my previous missions. And I will work very hard as your farm employee. I am greatly honored that you would accept me."

He then turned to Bert and said, "Mr. Sheriff, my expectation when I came to your office yesterday was that you would arrest me and eventually I would either be in jail for the rest of my life or I would be executed. Words cannot express how grateful I am to you. I will try and find some way to try and repay you for your trust."

The sheriff looked at General Park and replied, "No need. I'm just trying to do what is best for everyone. That's my job. As Gunsmoke said, welcome to the U.S. and to Harlan County!"

Chapter 27

The North Pacific
January 2

Captain Saito was relieving Second Officer Kozo Yamazaki at the helm. Kozo had departed for the head. The captain was staring intently ahead at another vessel about one mile off his port beam when the bridge door opened and Admiral Sung and Lt. Commander Shin walked in. Captain Saito glanced over his shoulder at them and said, "Good morning gentlemen."

The admiral said, "You've probably had better ones, Captain. I'm here to officially inform you on behalf of the North Korean government that we are taking command of this vessel."

Captain Saito released the helm and jerked his head around. He saw the admiral holding a pistol pointed toward him. He said, "What exactly are you doing?"

Admiral Sung said, "As I said, we're taking command of the ***Taka Maru***. I have stationed my men at all the critical locations and I would strongly advise you to cooperate with us. If you do, then no one will be harmed. If you do not, then I can assure you we will not hesitate to use whatever force is required. Do you understand?"

"I hear what you say," the captain said, "but I don't understand what you wish me and my crew to do."

"You do just what I say," the admiral said. "While we are capable of operating this ship, we would prefer that you and your crew continue to perform their duties as usual. We will tell you where to navigate and you will follow those instructions. Do you understand?"

"Yes," Captain Saito replied.

"So now get on the horn and tell your crew about the management change," Admiral Sung demanded.

Captain Saito reached for the microphone, held it to his mouth, and said, "Gentlemen, this is the captain speaking. I'm informing you that the military personnel from North Korea have taken command of the ***Taka Maru***. No one will be harmed if we simply do as they ask. Please cooperate with them."

Admiral Sung smiled and said, "Well done captain. Commander Shin has the coordinates for the course that you are to follow."

Shin gave the coordinates to the captain who then entered them into the ship's navigation system. They were now headed straight toward Los Angeles.

––––––––––

Mr. Cho heard the words of the captain over the ship's audio system. At the time he was resting in his cabin. It was just about the exact time that had been predicted.

There was a knock on his door. "Enter," Mr. Cho said.

In walked two of the North Korean soldiers. One said, "Mr. Cho, did you hear the announcement made by Captain Saito?"

"Yes, I heard it," replied Mr. Cho.

"Will you agree to carry on with your duties even though we have taken command of the ship?"

"Yes, I will," Mr. Cho said.

"Thank you," said the other soldier who made a check mark on the sheet he had held on a clipboard. Then he added, "Carry on." The two turned and left Mr. Cho's cabin.

Mr. Cho raised his watch close to his mouth and said, "The North Koreans are now in charge of the ship. Apparently everything went peacefully. So far, so good."

––––––––––

Two Hours Later

Admiral Sung, Lt. Commander Shin, their Chief Petty Officer, and Petty Officer First Class were meeting in the Belly Room. The other 8 soldiers were stationed at critical positions, with two of them holding at gunpoint Captain Saito and Second Officer Kozo Yamazaki on the bridge. The Captain and Kozo were only allowed to leave the helm to go to the head, and when that occurred one of the soldiers accompanied them. They would be required to alternate sleeping on the floor of the bridge.

Admiral Sung spoke, "Gentlemen, I'm happy to report that the takeover went without problems. The captain and second officer are being held on the bridge and are cooperating fully with us. We have canvassed all of the ship's crew and each has said they would cooperate. We have no reason to believe that our mission will not be accomplished. Each of you know your assignments, so without questions I ask that you continue with those. Our next major objective will be tomorrow morning when we begin to assemble the missile launch station. You are dismissed."

Washington, D.C.
The Pentagon

The two naval officers monitoring the audio from General O's watch looked at each other. One said, "That sounds like the bad guys have taken over the ship. I should probably inform Director Kennan."

The second officer replied, "Yeah, good idea. And tell him that General O said the transition went peacefully."

The North Pacific
USS Kentucky

The ***USS Kentucky*** (SSBN-737) is a nuclear United States Navy Ohio-class ballistic missile submarine commissioned in 1991. She carries a complement of 15 officers and 140 enlisted men. She was currently submerged at 300 feet, about 5 miles north of the ***Taka Maru,*** and moving in the same direction and at the same speed as the Japanese vessel.

Radio operator Pennebaker turned in his seat and spoke to Captain Key, "Sir, I just monitored a message from General O that said the ***Taka Maru*** was now under command of the North Koreans and that the takeover was accomplished without incident."

Captain Key replied, "Right on schedule. Good to know it went smoothly. Keep me posted, Pennebaker."

Harlan, Kentucky

Mayor Knapp and Sheriff Sterling were sitting together at a table in Creech Cafe having coffee. The mayor said, "Bert, it sure is a strange world. Who would have thought that the person who almost killed everyone at the Slusher brothers'

Christmas party just a little over a week ago would now be accepted as a friend and living with the very people he tried so desperately to kill?"

"You're exactly right, mayor," Bert replied, "and he even came back a second time to try and do the job. But like the other North Koreans, he was just a soldier following orders from his madman, nutcase leader. And he too seems like a truly good person. And that was not just my take, but the Slusher brothers thought the same. So he's now peacefully coexisting with his fellow countrymen at the Slusher farm. You're right....who would have thought it?"

Just then an ear-piercing cackle was heard from the back of the cafe. Bert and Fred turned to look and saw Mrs. Harrison doubled over laughing. Fred said, "Well, I see Mrs. Harrison spotted my latest posting.....and it is very funny."

Bert looked at Fred and said, "You gonna keep me waiting?"

Fred replied, "Nah, I'll tell it to you. The article was from the Louisville **Courier-Journal** and reported on an event that took place at the St. Anne convent in Newport, Kentucky. The Mother Superior called all the nuns together and told them that they had a case of gonorrhea in the convent. An elderly nun at the back stood up and said 'Well thank God. I'm so tired of chardonnay.'"

Bert roared with laughter. He reached over and slapped Fred on the back and said, "Fred, that's one of your better ones. That should keep me in a good mood for the rest of the day."

"Glad you enjoyed it, Bert," the mayor replied. "Any news at all from General O?

"Nothing," Bert replied. "Quiet as a mouse. Let's hope no news continues to be good news. I certainly do worry about him."

"Me too," Fred replied.

Chapter 28

The North Pacific
January 3

Admiral Sung and Commander Shin stood on deck the ***Taka Maru***. The admiral said, "Today the ship's crew will see the missile and start to put two and two together. It will be very important that they not know any of the details of our operation. They can guess, but that will be all."

Shin said, "Thus far things have gone very smoothly. I see no reason why that should not continue. Our men are well informed and have their orders."

Two North Korean soldiers then appeared on deck bringing Mr. Cho and Chief Engineer Fugio Tanaka. Admiral Sung said, "Welcome gentlemen. It is time to begin work on our project. Since the two of you were involved in operating the crane to load our containers we now need you to assist us by placing each one on deck as we direct. Once a container is placed on deck we will unload its contents and then direct you to bring us another one. Is that agreeable?"

Chief Tanaka said, "Yes, we can do that."

Admiral Sung then pointed to a container that rested atop one of the stacks and said, "Let's begin with that one." He then pointed to a location on the deck and said, "We want it placed at that spot."

Tanaka and Cho both nodded and started to walk toward the ship's crane. As they walked Mr. Cho said softly, "Chief, we'd best cooperate. I think failure to do so would likely result in harm coming to either our captain or one of our crew."

"I agree," the chief said as he started climbing the stairs leading to the cab of the crane. Once in the cab he took a seat and started the engine. Mr. Cho grabbed a loading strap and climbed the stack of containers until he reached the one identified by the admiral. He then secured the strap across the top of the container and gave a 'thumbs-up' sign to Tanaka.

The chief then swung the crane around and dropped its hook, expertly grabbing the loading strap on the selected container. He then raised the arm of the crane and rotated it until it was directly above its designated destination on deck. He then slowly lowered the cable that had the hook and container at its end. Mr. Cho carefully guided the container as soon as it was within his reach, and he gave the final 'thumbs down' sign to lower the cargo to the deck. The first container had been successfully moved.

Commander Shin and the two soldiers then moved with tools in hand to the container and removed screws on one side. The side was hinged at the bottom, and after the screws were removed the side was lowered as it rotated on its hinge, thus exposing the cargo inside. The two soldiers then walked into the container and removed screws that were attached to the boxed cargo to secure it in place. Then they pushed, one on each end, the box which rolled on casters on its bottom, out and over the lowered side onto the deck. They then rotated the container's hinged side back up and secured it in place with the previously removed screws.

The commander looked at Mr. Cho and said, "Okay, stow this empty container somewhere."

Mr. Cho looked up at Chief Tanaka and gave him the 'thumbs up' sign. He raised the empty container, moved it to the storage location, and lowered it. Mr. Cho walked over and removed the loading strap and the chief then raised the empty hook, ready for the next move.

The commander ordered the two soldiers to move the box to the side of the empty deck space and then said to the admiral, "Ready for number two."

Admiral Sung nodded and pointed to the next container.

The process was repeated until all five containers were unloaded. The last one was marked with the red 'caution' letters, and both the admiral and commander told the two crew members to use extreme caution and to move the container very, very slowly. Mr. Cho noticed beads of sweat on their faces. He knew this one contained the nuclear warhead.

When all containers were unloaded there were five boxes lined up side by side on the deck. The commander then asked that Mr. Cho and Chief Tanaka assist the two soldiers in unboxing the cargo. The first box was opened and inside were several large instruments. Mr. Cho thought these likely formed the control console for the missile. The second box contained a large base which Mr. Cho reasoned was the launch platform. The third, fourth, and fifth boxes contained the body of the missile. The third had the lower part with guiding fins attached, the fourth was simply a long fuel segment, and the fifth contained the cone-shaped top of the missile that housed the nuclear warhead.

After all the boxing had been removed, each of the five cargos remained resting on its base with casters for moving. The admiral then said, "Okay, that's good for right now. It's time for lunch. Be back here at 1330 promptly and we'll begin integrating the parts. You are dismissed."

The admiral, Lt. Commander, two soldiers, Chief Tanaka, and Mr. Cho were all reassembled on deck. Admiral Sung said, "Now we start the task of assembling. Let's begin with the contents of the first container."

The men all walked to the base upon which the instruments and other equipment lay. Under the direction of Lt. Commander Shin they carried all the parts from the base and sat them on the deck in a fringe area. In addition to the instruments there was a metal rack into which they could be mounted and a large roll of cable that apparently would be used to connect the control console to the missile.

The launch platform was next moved to an area approximately in the center of the deck. It was extremely heavy, and was moved on its base by having the four men push it to its approximate final location and then sliding it off its base onto the deck. Small movements as directed by Commander Shin were accomplished by all four pushing on one side. It was then in place.

The three missile segments were next off-loaded from their bases. This was accomplished by removing their restraining blocks and allowing the segments to roll off their bases onto the deck. This was easily accomplished for the middle section, the cross section of which was circular. The first section had fins around its lower section, but these were actually an aid to slowly roll it into place on the deck. The top of the missile, containing the nuclear warhead, was also easily, but very slowly and carefully, rolled onto the deck. The three sections had been constructed to fit together by simply pushing one into another. A special locking mechanism engaged when the sections were tightly assembled. Lining up the segments into a straight line took almost an hour, and was accomplished by very slowly rolling the segments until alignment was achieved. The difficult part was to then push the segments together. To do this an oil was sprayed on the deck where the segments rested, and then all four men would push one segment into the next until the locking mechanism could be heard to engage. Finally, after a total of almost three hours of manipulations, the missile was assembled, but lying horizontally on the ship's deck. It had to next be lifted to the vertical position and placed in the launch platform. This was accomplished by fitting a loading strap around the top of the missile and then using the crane to slowly raise it. As this was done a wooden 2X4 placed across the deck at the missile base with a soldier standing on each end prevented the bottom of the missile from moving. It was thus carefully moved to vertical. Once in the vertical position a rope harness that the North Koreans had brought with them was fitted over the missile. The bottom of the harness was attached to the fins on the missile's base and the top of the harness came to a point above the missile's forward tip. The crane's hook was then attached to the top of the harness and the entire missile lifted up, across to the launch platform, and then lowered until it was in place. The harness was then removed, and the missile was finally in position to be launched.

The assembled missile was almost thirty feet tall and weighed 3,000 pounds. The deck where it stood was forward of the bridge, from which Captain Saito and Kozo Yamazaki had been watching as it took its sinister appearance. The captain then looked at the second officer and said, "Lord help us."

Admiral Sung gathered the other five men together to the location of the control console and said, "Everything has gone splendidly thus far in our assembly operation. I thank each of you for your help and cooperation." He then looked at Cho and Tanaka and continued, "I know that you two crew members must be wondering about this missile. Please do not concern yourselves. At dinner tonight I plan to fully explain our plan. It is nothing for you to worry about." He then turned to Commander Shin and said, "Please now complete the assembly by setting up the control console and connecting it to the missile. After that you may dismiss the men. I'm going to my quarters."

"Yes admiral," replied the commander. He and the other two soldiers then began assembling the instruments into the control console rack. Cho and Tanaka simply handed them tools and gave them a hand in positioning the instruments. When that was completed they took the connector on one end of the roll of cable and inserted it into a receptacle on the back of the control console. The two crew members then assisted in unrolling the rest of the cable on the deck over to the launch platform, and plugged-in the connector on that end into the launch platform receptacle.

Commander Shin walked to the control console and connected the bank of four batteries hooked up in parallel to the instruments and said, "Okay, I'm going to check to see if all systems are operating." He then flipped the toggle switch that was labeled 'power' and all the instruments lit up. A large green 'ready' light glowed as did a red button on the right side of the console that had the word 'launch' on it. Shin smiled and said, "All systems are go. You are dismissed. See you for dinner, and thanks again for your help. The assembly is complete."

Mr. Cho and Chief Tanaka left the deck for their quarters. The chief said, "Mr. Cho, I sure don't know what they're up to, but it doesn't look good to me. You have any thoughts?"

Mr. Cho replied, "Not really. Maybe they'll share their plans at dinner tonight. I'm just in the dark on all this."

The two crew members reached their cabins. Mr. Cho said, "See you at 1800 for chow."

"You bet," the chief replied.

Mr. Cho closed the door to his cabin and sat on his bunk. He was pleased. The control console was very similar to the ones he had trained on, and he felt confident he understood the instruments and programming procedure for the missile. He had noted that there was a keyboard with a monitor directly above it, exactly like the ones he was familiar with. He recalled from his training that if the word 'program' was entered into the keyboard a screen would appear that allowed either target coordinates or target city airport codes to be entered. He anticipated that when the missile was about ready to be fired the city code for Los Angeles, *LAX*, would be entered. After this it would simply be a matter of pressing the red 'launch' button to fire the missile. His job would be to prevent that from happening. He then brought his watch up close to his lips and briefly stated what had transpired with the missile assembly, and then said he felt everything was good and that he would be able to prevent the launch as they had planned. He then lay down on his bunk to rest before dinner. He wondered what kind of tale the admiral would concoct to explain the presence of the missile. He'd find out at 1800.

Everyone except two soldiers and Second Officer Kozo Yamazaki were present on the mess deck for dinner. The second officer remained at the helm with the two soldiers guarding him. After everyone else had finished eating the admiral stood in the center of the room and said, "Gentlemen, I want to thank each of you for your cooperation. I know that you are curious about what's going on, and I intend to now tell you. As you are aware, the North Korean government seized this ship yesterday. Captain Saito and Officer Yamazaki have been held at gunpoint on the bridge. They have been steering the ship according to our coordinates, and have fully complied with our orders." He then pointed to Captain Saito seated at a nearby table and said, "As you can see, the captain has not been harmed." The captain nodded in agreement. The admiral continued, "My government has developed a new missile, one of which is currently in its launch platform on the foredeck of the *Taka Maru*. For reasons that I will not go into, the missile could not be test fired in our country. After much discussion and training it was decided to use a civilian vessel to transport the missile to a predetermined location for testing. In about four more days we will reach the desired location and will fire the missile. It is a modified 'cruise-type' missile that deploys close to the surface. When we reach our destination and launch it, the test, if all goes as expected, will not be detected by unfriendly forces. No one will be hurt, and as long as each of you continues to cooperate we will, at the conclusion of the test, immediately head back to Chongjin. Once there we will return command of the *Taka Maru* to Captain Saito and the North Korean government will compensate the OKN Line handsomely for the use of their ship. You will then be free to continue your normal operations. Is that clear?"

Heads either nodded in the affirmative or remained motionless. Captain Saito then said, "Admiral Sung, speaking on behalf of the crew I thank you for your explanation. We will continue our cooperation and look forward to the rapid conclusion of your operation."

The admiral smiled and responded, "Thank you captain." He then nodded to the soldier accompanying the captain. The two of them then stood and the captain was escorted back to the bridge. When there he briefed Kozo Yamazaki on the admiral's explanation of events. Their two guards remained in place.

Chapter 29

The North Pacific
January 4

The admiral and commander were sitting together in the belly room of the ***Taka Maru***. The admiral said, "Shin, what is your assessment of how things went yesterday?"

The commander replied, "I thought they could not have gone better. The missile assembly went without a hitch, and it checked out to be all ready to fire. Your explanation to the ship's crew was brilliant. It seemed they accepted it as perfectly logical, and I think each of them believe that we're just test firing a new missile at a location where our enemies will not be able to detect it. Congratulations, admiral!"

"Thank you commander. I too thought it was a good day. I reported to our supreme leader last night. He also was pleased and was greatly looking forward to his birthday present. And speaking of that, have you calculated the coordinates for the launch?"

"Yes," said Commander Shin, "as you know, we are currently cruising due east at 34 degrees north latitude, the same latitude as Los Angeles. We will continue until we reach a longitude of 135 degrees west. In order to fire the missile at exactly midnight on January 7th, just as our supreme leader's birthday arrives on January 8th in Pyongyang, we will need to be at the coordinates of 34 degrees north latitude and 135 degrees west longitude and launch at exactly 0630 local time on January 7th. At our current speed, and given that the weather conditions look very favorable, I see no problem arriving at the launch coordinates several hours prior to the launch time."

"That sounds fine," Admiral Sung said. "And then how long will the missile take to reach Los Angeles?"

Commander Shin responded, "That will be a 1000 mile flight, and should take about 90 minutes. At 0130 on January 8th in Pyongyang, which would be 0900 on January 7th in Los Angeles, the city will no longer exist."

"Supreme leader Kim will be delighted," said the admiral. "And then we must execute the ship's crew. We must leave no one to reveal our true mission. After that, we'll sail the **Taka Maru** back to Chongjin and our mission will be finished.

Mr. Cho had just completed making his rounds and had returned to his cabin. He sat on his bunk thinking about how the situation had developed yesterday. Everything was pretty much as expected. He felt confident he could defeat the launch. He knew that when it was time to fire the missile the admiral or commander would go to the launch station and enter the target coordinates. After this was done the red launch button would be pressed. This would start a five minute countdown to permit the personnel to clear the launch area. After exactly five minutes the missile would fire and could not be recalled or redirected. It would be on its way to Los Angeles. It was this five minute period after pressing the launch button that provided the opportunity to defeat the mission. Mr. Cho and all his advisors back in the U.S. had agreed that during this five minute period he would need to get to the control console and reprogram the missile to a target that was unreachable. They had chosen Auckland, New Zealand, whose three digit airport code was AKL. They reasoned that the missile would simply run out of fuel after about 1500 miles in flight and would fall harmlessly into the pacific ocean. The nuclear warhead would only detonate if and when the target coordinates were achieved. Between where the ship was located and Auckland was only water and a few isolated islands. The odds were extremely good that when the missile ran out of fuel it would simply sink into the depths of the South Pacific. Mr. Cho knew that everything depended on his being able to get to that control console, enter the word 'program', and then scroll to the airport code 'AKL' and hit 'enter' on the console keyboard. The missile would then be programmed to fly toward Auckland, New Zealand rather than Los Angeles. As he thought about this he realized that it would not be an easy task. He knew that the admiral and commander would immediately leave the launch area after pressing the launch button because of all the noise, fumes, and hot exhaust that would develop there. He reasoned they would likely go to the bridge and watch the launch from there. Likely one or two soldiers would be left to secure the launch area. He knew he would have to confront them prior to going to the control console. Since he didn't have much time, he had decided to try and get the chief engineer, Fugio Tanaka, to assist him. He and the chief had become good friends, and he felt he could trust him. He knew there were only about three more days until launch. He must find a time to discuss this with Chief Tanaka.

Washington, D.C.
The White House

Susan Bean, Director of National Intelligence, and President Dickson Cannon were meeting in the oval office. The president said, "Damn it Susan, I still don't like it! We're gambling millions of lives on that ex-North Korean general. If he screws up, Los Angeles is history. I know it sounds harsh and insensitive, but why not just push that button and blow that damn boat out of the water. No one would even know about it."

"We could do that Mr. President, but it would kill at least a couple dozen people and could conceivably even trigger the nuclear weapon. In any case, the world would learn about it because OKN Lines would certainly report one of its ships missing and it would eventually come out. But the most important factor to consider is the probability that General O will accomplish his mission is very, very high. Everything we planned is exactly on track. Nothing has gone wrong. I still say we should continue as planned and let the general do his thing."

"I still don't like it, but I guess you're right," replied the president. "But I want everything monitored very, very closely. If anything whatsoever goes wrong I want that ship blasted. Do you understand?"

"I do," replied Director Bean.

"One other thing," said the president, "If General O does his thing and the missile is fired at New Zealand, what then is going to happen to General O and the crew of the ship?"

Susan Bean said, "Good question! The moment the missile is fired a team of six navy seals will be launched from the **USS Kentucky**. It should take them no longer than about 15 minutes to arrive at the **Taka Maru**. They will board the ship and should be able to subdue the North Koreans and return command of the ship to Captain Saito in short order. And hopefully with no loss of life. The ship would then return to Ishigaki Port, Japan and the North Korean soldiers turned over to the Japanese authorities."

"And then I'd want the prisoners shipped over here for interrogation. We need to learn everything we can about that damn maniac Kim Jong-un and his nuclear threat," the president said.

Director Bean responded, "I agree."

"One last thing, Madame Director," said the president. "Tell me again why we can't just send in the seals now rather than wait until that damn missile is fired. If we could, that would eliminate the possibility of that missile going to Los Angeles."

"I understand your question, Mr. President," Susan Bean said. "The answer is that the navy gave that option due consideration and decided that there simply was too much of a chance that either the seals might be detected before boarding the ship or that if conflict developed after aboard there would be the chance that the North Koreans could fire the missile. The navy decided that it was far better to go the route we're going."

President Cannon said, "I see. But I still don't like it."

Chapter 30

The North Pacific

January 6

Mr. Cho was standing on the second level aft deck beside a large fan that distributed air throughout the **_Taka Maru_**. He had just summoned Chief Tanaka, telling him there was a problem with the fan.

"Hi Norio, what seems to be the problem?" asked the chief as he looked at the fan.

"Don't know," replied Mr. Cho. "It just seems to have stopped running."

Chief Tanaka started tracing the fan wiring and spotted a disconnected wire. Just as he started to speak Mr. Cho bent over beside him with his forefinger across his lips and quietly said, "I disconnected it. I just needed an excuse to talk with you without any chance of the soldiers hearing."

Fugio Tanaka looked a bit surprised and said, "Okay, I think it's safe to talk now."

Mr. Cho nodded and said, "Thanks! As you may have guessed, I'm not really an engineer. I work for a government that is concerned about the North Korean nuclear capability. The missile that now stands on our foredeck is armed with a nuclear warhead. It is my mission to prevent them from firing it. Should they be successful, I can assure you that millions of people will be killed by the nuclear explosion. I realize I'm taking a chance sharing this information with you, but I desperately need help, and I think I can both trust you and hopefully enlist your help."

Chief Tanaka looked somewhat shocked, but said, "I suspected something was fishy about that missile, and I also suspected something didn't add up about your background..... but I just kept my mouth shut. I've got to tell you that I now feel like a great weight has been added to my shoulders, but I'll certainly help you in any way I can. Exactly what did you have in mind?"

Mr. Cho replied, "All the information we have indicates that the launch is getting very close. We are almost certain it will occur sometime within the next 24 hours. When they're ready for launch they will stop the ship and then the admiral and commander will likely go to the control console to start the firing sequence. I have information that once that is done the missile will fire in five minutes. I think the two of them will then go to the bridge to observe the launch, but will likely leave one or two soldiers with the missile for security. I can misdirect the missile if I can get to the control console during that five minute period. I need your help to take care of the soldiers and allow me access to the console."

"I understand," replied the chief. "How do we coordinate this?"

Mr. Cho said, "I think the best way would be for us to meet in my cabin as quickly as possible after the ship comes to a stop. We should be able to both hear and feel the ship's forward progress stopping. When that happens we both come to my cabin and then we'll go together to the launch site. We'll have to assess the situation when we get there. Is that okay with you?"

"Sure," said Chief Tanaka. "Will we have any weapons?"

Mr. Cho replied, "No firearms, but I thought we'd each take a large wrench....real good for giving those soldiers a bad headache."

Chief Tanaka smiled and said, "I understand!"

They refastened the wire on the fan, closed up its control box, and each walked away in different directions.

January 7

Mr. Cho had not slept well. He knew today was launch day. His normal routine was to awaken around 0500, do his bathroom duties, have breakfast, and start his daily rounds at about 0600. He had just left the mess deck when the ship's engines stopped. He turned and hurried back to his cabin.

Chief Tanaka met Mr. Cho as he approached his quarters. The two entered the cabin. Mr. Cho opened a drawer and withdrew two very large pipe wrenches and handed one to the chief. They then left the cabin and started walking toward the launch deck.

Mr. Cho was very aware of where some of the soldiers were normally stationed, and avoided taking a route that would encounter them. They soon arrived at the launch site. Chief Tanaka trailed behind Mr. Cho, who carefully stuck his head around a corner to be able to view the launch area. He saw the admiral, the commander, and two soldiers standing beside the launch console. He saw the commander look at his watch and say, "We've got about 15 more minutes before the launch sequence. We'll hit the launch button at exactly 0625, and then at precisely 0630 the engine will ignite and the missile will be on its way."

The admiral said, "Good. Good. Everything looks fine." He then looked at the two soldiers and instructed each of them to stand guard, one beside the missile and the other beside the control console. He told them that exactly four minutes after the launch button was pressed they were to move to the rear of the ship. He then said to the commander, "I'm going on up to the bridge. After you initiate the launch sequence you come up and join me. It should be a good show from up there."

"Yes admiral," the commander replied.

The admiral then walked along the port rail to the ladder that went up to the bridge. Mr. Cho and Chief Tanaka were on the starboard side. Mr. Cho whispered to the chief, "As soon as the two soldiers leave their stations I'll make my move. You can just remain here to watch for any unwelcome visitors. I will have exactly one minute to reprogram the missile before launch. I'll move close along the wall over to the control console.....and shouldn't be visible from the bridge. We'll both need to get clear of the area before the missile fires. Okay?"

The chief gave a thumbs up and nodded affirmatively.

Commander Shin looked at his watch. He typed the word 'program' on the control console keyboard. The monitor showed an alphabetical list of international city airport codes. He scrolled down to LAX, corresponding to Los Angeles, and hit the enter key. The monitor then confirmed the target as Los Angeles, California, USA. The commander then looked again at his watch. He waited until exactly 0625, at which time he reached over and pushed the red launch button. A digital clock above the button started counting down from 5:00. The commander left the control console and started walking rapidly along the ship's port rail toward the ladder that went up to the bridge.

Mr. Cho said softly to Chief Tanaka, "The five minute countdown has started. I think the soldier guarding the console will leave along the port rail. I'm not sure if the one guarding the missile will leave port or starboard. If he elects to come to starboard we'll have to deal with him."

"I understand," replied Chief Tanaka.

After about two minutes had passed the guard at the base of the missile decided it was time to move. He elected to turn to the port side and starting running toward the rear of the ship. Several seconds later the guard on the control console started walking down the port side toward the back of the ship. When this happened, and as soon as the guard was out of sight, Mr. Cho started to trot along the wall over to the port side and then down the rail toward the control console. His path was blocked from view from the bridge due to containers stacked on the port side. He reached the control console and immediately typed in the word 'program'. He saw the list of airport codes appear on the monitor. What he didn't see was the last guard, who had apparently turned and looked back along the port rail and saw Mr. Cho at the console. The guard had turned and ran back toward the launch area. As he was approaching the console he shouted, "Hands up." Mr. Cho ignored him. He pulled his revolver, pointed it directly at Mr. Cho's chest, and fired two rounds. Before he could fire again a large pipe wrench crashed on his head, and he slumped to the deck. Chief Tanaka gave Mr. Cho a thumbs-up sign.

Mr. Cho felt extremely warm, and felt his chest. It was hot, and he noticed that the heat seemed to be radiating from the anchor cross he was wearing on the chain about his neck. He had felt the impact of the two bullets, but they seemed deflected, as if by some kind of shield.

He looked at Chief Tanaka and returned the thumbs-up sign, and then shouted to him "Run.....take cover!"

He looked at the digital clock above the red launch button and saw it was down to ten seconds. As he started scrolling through the international city airport codes looking for AKL he suddenly felt very dizzy. His vision started going black. He was losing consciousness. The last thing he remembered was pressing the enter key on the control console keyboard as he fell to the deck.

"Did you hear that? It sounded like gunfire," Admiral Sung asked commander Sin. The two were in the bridge with Captain Saito, Second Officer Kozo Yamazaki, and the two soldier guards.

"Yes, I heard it," replied the commander. "The missile's about to launch, it probably was a noise associated with it."

"I hope," said the admiral.

Just as he spoke the missile ignited. An ear-splitting roar erupted along with a blinding brightness that caused everyone to momentarily close their eyes. When they opened them they saw the exhaust from the missile spewing downward and deflected off the starboard side of the ship by the exhaust deflector in the launch platform. Smoke completely encompassed the front of the ship. And then the missile was gone....like a bolt of lightning. The admiral and commander quickly went out the bridge's rear door onto a small deck where they could look skyward. They saw the missile streaking to the east while maintaining an altitude of only about 400 feet above the water. In seconds it was out of sight.

"Supreme Leader Kim's birthday present has just been launched," said Admiral Sung with a big smile.

Washington, D.C.
The White House

The John F. Kennedy Conference Room is a 5525 square foot conference room and intelligence management center in the basement of the West Wing of the White House. It is commonly referred to as the Situation Room. The president was gathered there with all his National Security Council. They had been monitoring the audio from the watch worn by Mr. Cho.

"What the hell is going on?" the president asked.

CIA Director Kennan replied, "Sir, we just don't know. Everything seemed to be exactly on track until we heard those two gun shots. We've heard nothing more from General O, but from the sound of things the missile did fire. And that was confirmed from the **USS Kentucky**, which was at periscope depth and visually saw the missile leave the ship."

The president said, "Okay, but where is it going? Auckland or Los Angeles?"

Director Keenan replied, "We just don't know. At the altitude its flying we can't track it on radar. Hopefully we'll be able to hear from General O soon."

"In the meantime all the millions of people in Los Angeles could be getting ready to be blown off the face of the earth! Damn, damn, damn," said President Cannon. "If it's headed for LA what time will it get there?"

Director Susan Bean spoke up, "About 9 am local time, or noon here in D.C."

President Cannon said, "We don't even have enough time

to alert them. What could they possibly do in 90 minutes? It would just be mass confusion. Damn, damn, damn."

The North Pacific

Fugio Tanaka, shaking Norio Cho by the shoulders, said, "Norio, wake up....wake up".

Mr. Cho slowly rolled his head. He then barely opened his eyes. Then a sudden look of panic appeared on his face, and his eyes opened wide. He said, "What happened?"

Chief Tanaka said, "It looked like you passed out just before the missile launched. Were you able to change the code?"

Mr. Cho looked blankly at the chief and said, "I don't remember."

Seven North Korean soldiers suddenly appeared at the launch deck with guns drawn and pointed at Mr. Cho and Chief Tanaka. One said, "Hands on your head and follow us."

"Drop your weapons," came the voice from behind the soldiers. It was the familiar voice of Admiral Sung. The seven soldiers all turned in unison to see their leader with a gun held to each side of his head by two U.S. Navy seals. Seal #1 said, "Do exactly as he said and no one will be harmed. Drop your weapons, and do it NOW."

Seven guns fell to the deck.

"Now each of you sit and place your hands behind your backs," said seal #2.

Seal #1 gathered the weapons while seal #2 put cuffs on the soldiers, including Admiral Sung. Seal #1 then said to seal #2, "Go up to the bridge and bring all the others down here."

The other four Navy seals along with the remaining three North Korean soldiers, Commander Shin, Captain Saito, and Second Officer Kozo Yamazaki were retrieved from the bridge and brought to the launch deck.

Washington, D.C.
The White House

"Damn, Damn, Damn," said the president. "I heard that. That damn General O said he didn't remember if he changed the code! Now what do we do?"

"Calm down, chief, all the bad guys are captured....and no one got hurt. We'll find out shortly where the missile is going," Susan Bean said.

"I'm interested in Los Angeles," President Cannon said. "We're talking millions of people and World War III. I've got to know where that thing's going. I knew we should have blown up that ship!"

The Situation Room became quiet as a tomb.

Chapter 31

Washington, D.C.
The White House
January 7

President Cannon looked at his watch and said, "It's been over an hour since that damn missile took off, and we still don't have a clue where its headed. I want to talk directly with General O. Get him on the horn."

"Yes Mr. President," replied CIA Director Jon Kennan as he spoke into his cell phone. All others in the Situation Room were totally quiet.

The North Pacific
USS Kentucky

Radio operator Pennebaker turned to his captain and said, "Sir, we have a call from the White House wanting to speak with you."

Captain Key put on his headset and replied, "Put it through."

"Yes, this is Captain Key."

The president said, "Captain, this is President Cannon. I want to talk directly with General O. Can you patch me through to him?"

"I think so," replied the captain. "Please stand by Mr. President."

––––––––

The North Pacific
Taka Maru

All the prisoners were seated and cuffed on the foredeck. All the ship's crew, including Mr. Cho, were standing in back of the prisoners. The six Navy seals were standing with guns drawn in front of the others.

Seal #1 suddenly talked into his microphone, saying, "I'll put him on. Stand by." He removed his headset and said, "General O, you have a phone call."

Mr. Cho, aka General O, walked forward, took the headset

from Seal #1, placed it over his head and said, "Yes, this is General O."

"General, this is President Dickson Cannon. It's been over an hour since that missile was fired and we have no idea where its headed. Have you had any recovery of your memory? Do you recall anything at all about what you might have done to redirect it? Do you think its headed for New Zealand?"

"Mr. President, I still don't clearly remember. The last thing I recall was bringing up the program to change the missile's destination. It had been set for Los Angeles, and I remember starting to scroll to the Auckland code. Then I remember pressing the 'enter' key as I fell to the deck....out cold. My best guess would be that I may have changed the target code, but I honestly can't say for certain. And if I did change it, I don't know it's new target. I'm very sorry."

"We'll know shortly," said President Cannon. "God help us."

San Nicolas Island, California

The most remote of California's Channel Islands, San Nicolas Island is located in the Pacific about 75 miles west from Los Angeles. It is controlled by the United States Navy and is used for weapons testing and training. Local time there was 8:50 am.

A Navy jet was flying just west of San Nicolas when the pilot spotted it. It looked like a meteor streaking from the west, and it was coming at a low altitude....directly toward San Nicolas Island. The pilot called his base on the island and said, "There's a UFO streaking directly toward you out of the west. It's flying at a very low altitude. Should reach you momentarily."

The call was received by a naval radioman located in the small airport tower on San Nicolas Island. He alerted a couple of other people stationed there with him and they all looked out the tower toward the west. It happened so fast they could hardly identify it, but their prior military training suggested strongly that the large object that just streaked overhead at a high rate of speed was a missile, likely of the Tomahawk class. The tower operator immediately called his superiors.

Washington, D.C.
The White House

Director Jon Kennan's face turned white as a ghost as he heard the news on his cell phone. He turned to the president and said, "Mr. President, I just received a call reporting an incoming missile over San Nicolas Island, just west of Los Angeles, only moments ago. It was headed due east."

The deadly quiet of the Situation Room was broken by President Cannon's reply, "Only moments to go.....May God be with us."

San Gabriel Mountains, California

Just east of Los Angeles is a mountain range called the San Gabriels, the highest peak of which is Mount San Antonio, commonly referred to as Mt. Baldy. Sam and Susan had been hiking the trails of Mt. Baldy, and had spent the night in a tent on the mountain. They had just gathered all their equipment and started their journey toward the peak. Sam looked at his watch and said, "It's just after nine, we should be able to get close to the peak before noon."

Just then they spotted it. A sight nothing like they had ever seen. It looked like a giant Roman candle coming up the mountain at a terrifically high speed, but maintaining its low altitude, flying parallel with the mountain side. It zoomed directly overhead very loudly, and they could now even smell it's exhaust fumes. And then it was gone.

Mormon Lake, Arizona

Just southeast of Flagstaff, Arizona is a small lake named after the Mormon settlers who arrived there in the 1870s. The water in Mormon Lake fluctuates greatly, going from a depth of about 10 feet in the rainy season to near marsh during dry periods. Charlie and George loved to fish. They lived in Flagstaff, but came to Mormon Lake to fish for northern pike at every opportunity. This morning found them fishing very close to the bank on the eastern edge of the lake. The sandy land sloped steeply up from the water's edge to a peak about 50 feet high.

George reached over for his thermos and said, "Well, Charlie, those northern pike are hiding from us again. Might as well have another cup of mud." Just as he started to pour coffee from the thermos there was a strange sound of something rushing through the air and a huge black shadow passed over them. George dropped his cup and said, "What the hell was that?"

The two men then turned and looked at the sandy bank rising to their east and saw it. Only about a thousand feet from them, stuck in the sandy bank, was what looked exactly like a missile. The front part was buried in the sand, with about 25 feet sticking out at an angle of around 45 degrees. Smoke was still coming from its exhaust.

George looked at Charlie and said, "Damnest thing I ever did see. What'd you make it to be, Charlie?"

"Sure looks to me like some kind of rocket. Could be dangerous.....maybe we better get the hell out of here!"

"I'm calling 911," George replied as he pulled his cell phone from his pocket.

———

Flagstaff, Arizona

The dispatcher said, "911, what is your emergency?"

"You ain't gonna believe it, but a big damn rocket just landed right beside us here at Mormon Lake."

The dispatcher replied, "Sir, have you been drinking?"

"No," George replied.

"Taking drugs," asked the dispatcher?

"Hell no," said George. "I know it sounds goofy, but there's a big-assed rocket stuck in the sand right beside our boat here at Mormon Lake."

The dispatcher replied, "Sir, if I give you a phone number could you shoot a picture of it with your cell phone and send it to me?"

"Sure," George replied.

Washington, D.C.
The White House

Director Kennan quickly answered his ringing cell phone. Suddenly his face lit up like a lamp. He threw up his hands and shouted, "Thank you Jesus!! Just got word that the missile landed without exploding near a lake outside Flagstaff, Arizona."

The Situation Room erupted. Everyone jumped to their feet and starting shouting and dancing. President Cannon said, "I know that's the best news I ever received! Thank the Lord!"

Susan Bean said, "Mission accomplished! We'll get some people right out to that missile to secure it. I'm sure our military and intelligence will want to carefully inspect it."

President Cannon then said to Director Kennan, "Jon, get General O on the horn again for me."

The North Pacific
Taka Maru

Navy seal #1 smiled as he again removed his headset and said, "General O, it's the president again.....and he sounds a lot happier this time!"

General O put on the headset and said, "Yes, Mr. President."

"Congratulations General, that damn missile landed in Arizona without exploding. No one hurt. Your country owes you big time. I hope you'll do me the honor of visiting at the White House when you return."

General O had a hard time controlling his emotions. He simply stuck out his left hand with thumb raised high and all the ship's crew and the Navy seals started celebrating. The North Koreans sat glumly. General O finally said to the president, "Sir, it would indeed be a great honor to visit with you, but I must tell you that I had all kinds of help. And I still don't know exactly how I changed the target city."

"Don't matter one damn bit," said the president. "You're a national hero. You take care, have a safe trip home, and I'll look forward to meeting you."

Tears rolled down his face as General O said, "Thank you Mr. President!"

He collapsed into a chair beside the control console. Everything that had happened had been almost too much for him. He sat with his face in his hands, trying to control his emotions. Fugio Tanaka walked over to him, put his hand on his friend's shoulder and said, "Mr. Cho, I certainly don't know everything involved here, but one thing I do know.... you've just saved the lives of millions of people. I'll always cherish that you asked me to help you. I've now got a really, really good story to tell my grandkids!"

General O looked up at his friend, nodded affirmatively, and said, "You sure do, chief. And you be sure to tell them that I would not have accomplished my mission without you. Thank you so much!"

The missile ignition blast had knocked the control console over on its side. Everyone had assumed it was now nonfunctional. As General O sat in the chair he glanced over at it. He couldn't believe his eyes. He turned his head sideways to read the still functioning monitor:

LEX
Target:
Lexington, KY, USA

He smiled as he now realized what had happened. He wasn't able to scroll to AKL, but had just moved the target city from LAX to LEX before striking the 'enter' key and collapsing to the deck. The missile had been on track to Lexington, Kentucky when it ran out of fuel in Arizona

Chapter 32

Washington, D.C.
The White House
January 30

It was Monday morning. President Cannon, Jon Keenan, and Susan Bean sat together in the oval office for their weekly briefing.

The President said, "I want you two to know how absolutely delighted I am with the outcome of the Oak Ridge project. I don't have to tell you how close we came to World War III and to losing the lives of millions of Americans. That General O should go down in history right next to George Washington. Unfortunately, too many facts about what really happened will never be known to the public due to being classified. I still can't believe that the press didn't pick up on the missile being nuclear....although there was really no reason for them to think that. I guess that picture the fisherman took with his cell phone showing it sticking in the side of that Arizona hill could wind up as popular as the one of the six U.S. marines raising the American flag over Iwo Jima."

Director Bean said, "Yeah, it sure could. It's been plastered on the front page of every newspaper and magazine around the world, and on all the television programs. I'm sure even our friend Kim Jong-un saw it."

"No doubt," replied the president. "I understand from our sources that Kim executed three North Korean soldiers that he associated with the dozen that went on the mission. I think they were involved in training that group."

Director Keenan replied, "Yes, that's the word we got. He really got mad as hell when his birthday present turned out to be a dud! It's very fortunate for them that the Japanese government accepted the twelve North Korean soldiers for political asylum. If they had not, then Kim would have had them all executed when they returned home. And he would likely have done it in a very public way....like hanging them in the middle of Pyongyang."

"Speaking of them," said the president, "did our intelligence people have enough time to fully debrief them?"

Susan Bean responded, "Yes, the team was sent to Japan and stayed there for two weeks interrogating them. Since they were granted political asylum they were very cooperative, and appeared to answer fully all our questions. We gained a lot of knowledge about the North Korean nuclear program from them"

President Cannon said, "And a lot more from going over that damn missile, I'm sure."

"Yes," replied Director Keenan. "It was removed from the hillside and very carefully transported to Wright-Patterson Air Force Base at Dayton, Ohio for careful examination. It was, as we suspected, from Russia. It had been modified quite a bit for its mission. Based upon the information we gained from it we have now put into effect defensive measures that should prevent any future such missions from being successful."

"That makes me sleep a lot better," said the president. "That damn dictator just about pulled it off. Who would have thought he would do such a fool thing?"

"We sure had a lot of really good cooperation," replied Director Bean. "The Japanese government and the OKN Line were just super, and the crew of the **Taka Maru** cooperated wonderfully."

"They did, and we compensated them handsomely," replied President Cannon. "But nothing came even close to the amazing job of General O. I enjoyed so much my meeting last week with him. I was really sorry to inform him that so much of his miraculous mission must remain classified. But being the real trooper that he is, and with all his military training, he seemed to fully understand, and said that was perfectly okay with him and it was as it should be. Such a very fine fellow."

"Did you discuss with him why he passed out just as he was reprogramming the missile?" asked Director Keenan.

"We did talk about that," the president replied. "He said it was just a very strange thing. He said that everything was fine until that North Korean soldier fired the two shots at him. He explained that somehow the anchor cross that he was wearing protected him from sure death from those bullets. He said they miraculously just seemed to bounce off him. Really strange....he said he could feel the impact, but that they did no damage.....just bounced right off him. He attributed that to the strange and unexplained power of the anchor cross he was wearing. He said after that happened he only had about 20 seconds left to get the missile reprogrammed, and that he just suddenly started to pass out. He said after thinking about it he believes that the stress he was under just became too much, and his systems started to shut down. He could remember that he started to scroll through the airport codes as he blacked out, and he did also remember that he hit the 'enter' key on the keyboard before slumping to the deck. Very, very fortunately for us he changed the target from Los Angeles to Lexington, Kentucky. We came within a hair of the unspeakable happening."

Director Bean said, "Another incident that no one will ever know about is that Captain Key on the **USS Kentucky** came extremely close to pressing the button that would have exploded the **Taka Maru**. He said that when he was monitoring General O's audio from his watch and heard the two gun shots that he was almost certain the general was a goner. He said he hesitated just a few seconds and then heard the general responding to Chief Tanaka when he shouted 'Run......take cover!'. Had he not heard him, he would have pressed the button."

"Yet another example of how fortunate we were," replied President Cannon.

"What about the missile control console?" asked the president. "Did we get it?"

Jon Kennan replied, "Yes, we did. When the *Taka Maru* arrived back in port at Ishigaki a couple of our intelligence people already there to interrogate the North Korean soldiers went aboard the ship and retrieved the console. It was shipped to Wright-Patterson and was examined along with the missile."

"Good," President Cannon said. "Again, I'm just so pleased with all aspects of the Oak Ridge Project. Please convey my compliments to all your people that worked on it."

The two directors nodded in agreement.

Susan Bean then asked, "So, Mr. President, is General O well situated now in Kentucky?"

The president smiled, and with a twinkle in his eyes said, "He sure is. Just as soon as he arrived back in Japan our private jet picked him up and flew him back to Knoxville. Agents Clair Eaton and Rose McKay were there to meet him, and drove him to the Slusher Farm in Harlan, Kentucky. I understand word had leaked to the folks in Harlan that the general was on his way, and they all gave him a grand homecoming celebration upon his arrival. I might add that I made arrangements for him to receive a very nice yearly stipend from Uncle Sam for his tremendous duty to our country. Although he is now in great shape financially, he told me during our visit that he intends to remain and work at the Slusher Farm among his good friends for the remainder of his days. He is indeed an amazing man."

The two directors nodded vigorously in agreement.

Harlan, Kentucky

It was midafternoon. Sheriff J. Bert Sterling and Chief Deputy Kyle Potter were in Creech Cafe having coffee with Mayor Fred Knapp.

The mayor said, "Guys, I guess by now everything at the Slusher Farm is about back to normal."

Bert replied, "I think so, Fred. They were all so happy to have General O back safe and sound. I understand in talking with Gunsmoke that the Slusher Brothers are going to build another home on their property just for General O. I think they're planning to break ground for it in early spring. And, as you know, in the meantime he's bunking with General Park. Talk about strange bedfellows, rooming with someone who just about a month ago tried twice to kill him and everyone else at the Christmas party. But I understand that they hit it off real good, and everything is working out greatly for everyone. So I guess all's well that ends well!"

Fred replied, "Yeah, guess so. Hey Kyle, did he give you back your anchor cross?"

Kyle said, "He sure did. He caught me in a corner at his homecoming celebration and reached up and took off its necklace. He handed it to me, and with tears in his eyes told me how much it had meant to him and that it had indeed saved his life. He said without it many millions of people would have been killed. He then said he really couldn't tell me more than that, but he wanted me to know how very special it was and that his mission would not have been accomplished without it."

"Wow," Fred said. "That must have been some mission! You guys think it had anything to do with that missile that landed in Arizona?"

"Don't know," the sheriff replied. "Could have. It happened about the same time. But we didn't get many details about it, mostly we just got that amazing picture."

Fred said, "Got to tell you guys the latest one I heard this morning."

Bert and Kyle each smiled and nodded.

Fred continued, "A Polish guy went to the DMV to apply for a driver's license. They told him he had to first pass an eye exam. The optician showed him a card with the letters

CZWIXNOSTACZ.

The optician asked him if he could read the card. The Polish guy said, 'Read it? I know the guy'."

Bert and Kyle roared with laughter. Bert then said as he and Kyle stood, "Fred, once again you send us on our way with a smile on our face. Thank you my friend!"

9 780692 826874